infid/elity

stacey may fowles

ecw press

Published by ECW Press
2120 Queen Street East, Suite 200,
Toronto, Ontario, Canada M4E 1E2
416-694-3348 / info@ecwpress.com

LIBRARY AND ARCHIVES CANADA
CATALOGUING IN PUBLICATION

Fowles, Stacey May, author
Infidelity : a novel / Stacey May Fowles.

ISBN 978-1-77041-141-8 (PBK.)
ALSO ISSUED AS: 978-1-77090-432-3 (PDF);
978-1-77090-433-0 (EPUB)

I. Title.

PS8611.O877165 2013   C813'.6
C2013-902483-2

Editor for the press: Jennifer Hale
Cover and text design: David Gee
Scissors: © RedDaxLuma/DepositPhotos
Author photo: Lisa Kannakko
Typesetting: Carolyn McNeillie
Printing: United Graphics 5 4 3 2 1
PRINTED AND BOUND IN THE UNITED STATES

The publication of *Infidelity* has been generously supported by the Canada Council for the Arts which last year invested $157 million to bring the arts to Canadians throughout the country, and by the Ontario Arts Council (OAC), an agency of the Government of Ontario, which last year funded 1,681 individual artists and 1,125 organizations in 216 communities across Ontario for a total of $52.8 million. We also acknowledge the financial support of the Government of Canada through the Canada Book Fund for our publishing activities, and the contribution of the Government of Ontario through the Ontario Book Publishing Tax Credit and the Ontario Media Development Corporation.

For J, because we had a deal.

Perhaps all romance is like that;
not a contract between equal parties
but an explosion of dreams and desires
that can find no outlet in everyday life.
Only a drama will do and while the fireworks last
the sky is a different colour.

Jeanette Winterson, *The Passion*

Anything or anyone that does not
bring you alive is too small for you.

David Whyte

They say it takes a lot of nerve to leave someone at the altar. To call it off or
just simply not show up. I say that's bullshit. I say it takes a lot more nerve
to show up. It takes a lot of nerve to try to do anything that normal.

The safe thing always is to run. To just assume you're too fucked up
to do anything that remotely resembles normal. The good wife. The dot-
ing father. The safe thing to do is to be satisfied with being abnormal. To
accept being fucked up. And to be alone in your abnormality and fucked-
uppedness. To know that you are bad and alone and there's no fixing it or
even wanting to. To not do the work.

I was sitting on our back porch, smoking a cigarette, which is signifi-
cant because I don't even really smoke anymore, in fact I only ever smoked
when I was with Charlie, but I knew I wanted to smoke that day, and so
I did. I was sitting on our back porch, surrounded by the potted flowers
Aaron had diligently planted and cared for in anticipation of our backyard
wedding, smoking cigarette after cigarette, and I started to think about
how normal—how healthy—I had become without even meaning to do so.

Preparing to become the good wife. I was thinking about how I had quit everything bad, as if crossing off items on a list of everything that I enjoyed, and how I had started doing absurd things like eating organic, taking folic acid, and running, and how I had done all of those things for Aaron. In the name of being good. Good enough.

When I first met Aaron I was drunk on Jäger shots at a bar, and my drunkenness had made me charming and malleable, delightful even, and he went home with me that night and told me I was beautiful and exciting. He told me he wanted to take care of me. I think that was actually the last time I was drunk on Jäger shots. Everything I knew that made me who I was, every last filthy habit, fell apart because he willed it so. He never asked, but I liked him, even loved him, and I wanted to be better. It took me forever to do so, at least a couple of years, but I did it. I stopped smoking, stopped drinking, stopped sleeping until noon and eating red meat. I cut out sugar and the occasional line of cocaine. I stopped wearing makeup. I stopped wearing short skirts. I whitened my teeth.

I stopped kissing strangers.

I always loved kissing strangers.

I was very good at kissing strangers.

I stripped off so many things, so many layers of bad behaviours and filthy habits, that I started to forget who I was. What was I if I wasn't reckless? Who was I if not my vices, my foibles, my faults? I was a cardboard cut-out of a girl sitting on an IKEA folding chair on a back porch, with gleaming white teeth and no makeup.

So it was a week before the wedding, and I bought a pack of smokes. I knew while I was doing it that it meant more than I was pretending it did. The nice lady at the Korean grocer at the end of our street looked at me strangely when I asked for them.

"But you don't smoke," she said.

"They're not for me."

"Wedding soon! Excited?"

"Very."

Was I embarrassed or taking pleasure in lying? About the cigarettes or the wedding? I loved lying. I loved the thrill of having a secret you couldn't, didn't have to share with someone else. Aaron loved that we "have no secrets between us." Loved that we "tell each other everything."

When I got home I slowly peeled the cellophane off the box, and I pulled a cigarette out. I stared at it longingly and realized that it was a week until we were going to be married, and I needed more than just the cigarette. I needed wine. I needed to be wearing lipstick. I needed to call a random ex-boyfriend and ask him if he was still in love with me.

When I was self-destructive I was never afraid, but as Aaron helped me work my way toward "healthy" I became terrified of everything. When you are not willing death by your own hand, you're terrified it's going to jump out at you from every angle. Killer bees, left-turning buses, botulism. Aaron took care of me, but in doing so he ripped wide open a world that sought to destroy me. I was much more comfortable destroying myself.

So I put on red lipstick and poured myself a glass of red wine and smoked a cigarette and another cigarette, and a week before we were due to be wed, I knew I would leave him.

CHAPTER ONE

Ronnie knew the moment she saw Charlie that she would follow
him somewhere. It didn't really matter where, she just knew it would
happen sooner or later—that one day she would desert everything
important and chase him down. And that somehow it would be
worth it.

Ronnie wasn't the kind of girl who had ever felt that way about
anyone. Ronnie was the kind of girl who rarely felt anything. Since
she was young, Ronnie had always been quite skilled at numbing
herself to external influence.

She was wearing a short black strapless dress and open toed
shoes despite the fact that it was the middle of a Toronto December.
Her legs were bare, and every time the front door on the two-storey
Annex house swung open to let in another reveller she would shiver
slightly. Ronnie never dressed this way, generally wore blue jeans,
beat-up brown boots, T-shirts and cardigans, but Aaron had asked
her to dress up. She had styled her short brown hair, when normally

she would have simply let it dry after the shower. She had put on perfume, from an old bottle she found in the back of the medicine cabinet behind a row of prescription medication—a bottle that was a gift from Aaron two Christmases ago.

The party, a university affair full of scholars and students and assholes, twinkled with tinsel and blinking white lights. Everyone betrayed the slightest hint of discomfort, straining to have conversations with people they couldn't conceal their contempt for. They were drinking heavily to ease into the situation, and as the night wore on discomfort evolved into inappropriateness. Ronnie felt the burning stare of lechery on the hem of her dress and the curve of her cleavage.

Standing alone, far from the mistletoe that was trapping and tormenting some of the female guests, Ronnie tipped back a third glass of red wine and lamented agreeing to come.

Three glasses of wine meant she was drunk.

She had come for Aaron, who had needed her help carrying the many platters of food he'd prepared for the party. It was money, and they needed money more than ever now. Aaron was firmly set in "planning for the future" mode and was taking every extra catering job that came his way, even if it meant Ronnie had to assist.

"You'll have a great time, Ronnie, I promise. These are smart people. Like, smart famous people."

Ronnie wondered if there was such a thing as "smart famous people." The glossy pages of the magazines at the hair salon where she worked always suggested otherwise.

When her glass was empty again and she decided to go for a fourth, she saw him across the room. Through the maze of tweed coats, pencil skirts, and loud Christmas cheer, she spotted him slowly chewing something and staring blankly into the bottom of his whisky tumbler. He was a robust, rosy, bearded man with a slightly timid and mostly awkward look on his face. He looked decidedly lost, as if he might get swept away by the bumping shoulders of stodgy academics and earnest doe-eyed students. Despite his confused expression, it appeared that all eyes were on him. Ronnie overheard people whispering about him with a sense of awe, glad to be in his company yet afraid to approach him.

He was scanning the titles on a bookshelf while an angular and severe-looking blonde with a blunt-bang haircut and red-rimmed glasses was talking at him without any concern that he was paying attention. He looked up from the last drops of his whisky mournfully, as if it were the last whisky available in the world, and caught Ronnie in a stare. It should have been awkward, should have made her blush, turn on her heel, and clip off to the kitchen, but he seemed to derive so much pleasure from the eye contact that his mouth spread into a wide, welcoming grin immediately, and hers did the same.

The look on his face, his slight eye roll referring the blonde—in that moment she knew that he would have the capacity to make her do stupid things.

She put her wineglass down on a coffee table carelessly, without a coaster (a party grievance Aaron had warned her against), and, walked boldly toward him. Ronnie wasn't generally shy, but in situations where she had to be on her best behaviour because Aaron's job demanded it, she made careful exceptions to her generally animated personality. But for some reason this man and his canapé seemed a safe bet. When he saw her approaching, he raised a hand to excuse himself from the angular blonde, gesturing in Ronnie's direction in a way that suggested they had met before.

For some reason Charlie thought to put his left hand in his pocket so Ronnie wouldn't see his wedding ring as she approached.

Harmless, he thought.

He had a few brief moments to lament the mustard stain on the left breast pocket of his beige long-sleeved shirt, a shirt that his wife had picked out for him that morning.

"It's so good to see you again," he said at full volume.

"Don't worry, I don't think she can hear you anymore," Ronnie said in a half whisper, looking over his shoulder at the blonde. "She looks really fascinating."

"That's Sarah. She's a wench. And sort of my boss. I told her you were an old friend," he said.

"Well, maybe I will be."

"Charlie," he said.

"Ronnie," she said.

"Ronnie?"

"Veronica."

"Pretty."

Pretty.

They shook hands lightly. Then, reaching into his pocket with his right hand, he withdrew an oatmeal cookie.

"Why do you have an oatmeal cookie at a cocktail party?" she asked.

"I brought it with me. You can get all sorts of things from the fish at these things. Botulism. Ebola. Scabies," he said. "And who calls them cocktail parties anymore? What, were you born in the twenties?"

"Were you?"

"Ouch. Are you mocking me?"

"It's not hard. You smuggled in an oatmeal cookie in your pants pocket."

"And you can have half."

He carefully unwrapped the cookie and split it in two, handing her the bigger half. When he bit into and realized it was actually oatmeal with chocolate chips he playfully told her he wouldn't have offered it to her if he'd known. "A waste of good chocolate," he called it. She smiled and snatched the remainder of his half from his hand and shoved it, along with her half, into her mouth with both hands.

"Naw you haf nuffin," she said with her mouth full. Cookie crumbs tumbled from her lips and onto the front of the black dress Aaron had made her wear. He looked at her mouth, full of half-chewed cookie, and wanted to kiss it. He reached out to brush the cookie crumbs from the front of her dress but quickly stopped himself.

Things they would find out later:

He was more than ten years older than her.

She was an Aries and he was a Leo.

She knew what that meant and he didn't.

She cut hair for a living and looked in the newspapers for her horoscope every day.

He wrote poetry and she did not.

"So what brings you to this party then, Ronnie?"

"I know the caterer. You know, the one who prepared the scabies fish that you're so afraid of."

You know, the one I share a bed with, she thought.

Three and then four drinks in, with Aaron in the adjacent room, she suddenly longed for the thickness of Charlie's flesh, the width of his chest to curl into, the breadth of his arms around her, warming the skin exposed by strapless dresses and open-toed shoes. Admittedly this was not an uncommon occurrence for Ronnie, as alcohol always made her want to fall into strangers.

"We should do shots," she said.

"I'm close to fifty, Ronnie. I don't drink shots."

"Yawn."

"It's called being a 'grown-up.'"

"Again. Yawn. How close to fifty?"

"Close enough."

"Don't worry, old man. We'll just do girl shots."

"Girl shots?"

Ronnie flagged down one of the party's servers, a petite blonde whose buttery flesh was both awkwardly and sensually spilling out of an ill-fitting waistcoat, and exuberantly requested two B-52s. The girl, clearly out of her element, stared at her blankly.

"I don't think we . . ."

"Peach schnapps? Can you do that?" Ronnie suggested.

The blonde nodded and scurried off to the kitchen.

"Peach schnapps? What are we? Teenage girls at Bible camp?" Charlie asked.

"O-M-G Charlie. L-O-L."

"By the way, nobody orders shots at a cocktail party."

"Oh, Charlie. No one ever calls it a *cocktail party*."

"Touché."

The shots arrived and they drank them, toasting "Bible camp" and "a time when they called them cocktail parties" while the other party-goers eyed them strangely, their faces still expressing a strange awe over a man Ronnie knew nothing about. Ronnie was swaying now, the liquor impeding her balance and increasing her volume. Also warmed and buoyed from the inside, Charlie suddenly told Ronnie that her hair was nice. *Pretty*, he said.

"There's that word again," she said.

"Well it is. Pretty. It's shiny. Very Vivien Leigh. Natalie Wood. Elizabeth Taylor."

"Well, you mean young Elizabeth Taylor, I should hope."

"Bloated, wheelchair Elizabeth Taylor."

"Hey. Also, don't be awful."

"Don't be silly. *A Place in the Sun*, Elizabeth Taylor."

"Does that make you Montgomery Clift?"

"God, I hope so."

"You like old movies, then?"

"Oh yes. Simpler time. They don't make them like that anymore."

"The movies or the women?

"Both."

Ronnie could take a doctor's pressing questions much better than she could take compliments. She looked at her shoes and then back at Charlie. In doing so she noticed a chocolate chip cookie crumb still lingered in the corner of his mouth. She reached out to wipe it away and then, like him, stopped herself, realizing it was too intimate, her hand hovering between them.

"Cookie," she said by way of explanation, motioning toward the corner of her mouth.

"I'm sorry, did you just call me *Cookie?*" Charlie smiled and wiped the crumb away himself.

The angular blonde returned suddenly, obviously deviously curious about the identity of Charlie's young companion. "Charlie, there are lots of people you need to be meeting tonight," the woman said, momentarily ignoring Ronnie's presence.

"Yes, you've mentioned that a number of times, Sarah."

"You're not just here for the drinks, you know," she snapped back.

"Well, they don't even have B-52s."

Sarah ignored him and turned her attention to Ronnie. "Who's your friend? A student of yours?"

"This is Elizabeth. She's an actress. But don't bother talking to her. She doesn't speak any English," Charlie said without pause.

Ronnie attempted to stifle her drunken laughter while the blonde stared angrily at them both, quite aware that she was being lied to.

"Oh, I meant to ask you—how's your wife, Charlie?" Sarah asked. His grin quickly faded. Ronnie turned away from them slightly, wishing she had bothered to refill her wine glass.

"Tamara's doing very well. Thank you for asking."

"Oh, and your son? Noah? How is his treatment going? Elizabeth, are you aware that Charlie has a very sick child at home? He's such a devoted husband and father—oh I'm sorry, how rude of me. You can't understand a word I'm saying, can you?" Sarah was being cruel now, clearly intent on ruining Charlie's good-natured flirtation.

"Noah's not 'very sick,' Sarah. He has autism," Charlie spat, suddenly too offended to be embarrassed.

"Well, I do know it's been quite the struggle for the two of you. You and *your wife*."

"That's enough."

"You've had enough. I suggest you excuse yourself."

"I should get a refill," Ronnie offered, meekly trying to diffuse things.

"Yes. Maybe you should," Sarah retaliated.

"No. Ronnie, you stay. Sarah? If you could excuse us?"

"Please remember that you are here on behalf of the department."

Sarah exhaled noisily and then offered a dramatic exit, throwing Ronnie a mocking, loud, and slowly sounded out *sooo niiice tooo meeet you* before scurrying off to a more accommodating conversation elsewhere.

Ronnie gazed toward the kitchen, visibly uncomfortable. "Maybe I should go get that refill."

"I think she told me I should go, and as much as I'm loath to admit it—too much whisky I'm afraid," he said, again looking deep into his tumbler.

"No such thing," she said, raising her shot glass.

"I'm likely embarrassing you."

"I think I may be embarrassing myself. And the caterer."

"Please don't be put off by her. I told you she was a wench."

She smiled. "Maybe it's for the best if the fish gives everyone botulism."

"Ronnie, would you like to run away with me?"

"Where are we going?"

"I don't really care. Away from all of these godawful people."

"All these godawful people you're supposed to be meeting tonight?"

She looked around the room and, after deciding no one was eyeing them, she stepped forward, lightly pressing her body against him while slipping her empty shot glass into the same pocket the plastic-wrapped cookie came out of. She let her hand linger briefly inside the pocket before pulling away. He panicked slightly, but then eased into the moment letting his clumsy fingertips graze the hem of her dress, and then the outside of her bare thigh. Then the inside of her bare thigh.

"I'd like to see you again. Please," she whispered.

"Yes."

When she stepped back they both noticed the blonde staring.

"I should go find that caterer I'm embarrassing."

"We should run away."

"I should go find the caterer."

"Okay, then I suppose I should go find my wife. At home. It was nice to meet you Ronnie."

She had already turned away.

CHAPTER TWO

"Who was that you were talking to out there?" Aaron asked when Ronnie pushed through the swinging doors of the kitchen and desperately scanned the room for more peach schnapps.

"Some old guy," was her nervous response.

"I think he's supposed to be important or something. Like they're having this party for him."

"He didn't mention that."

"Couldn't you tell by the way all of them are staring at him?"

"I didn't really notice."

"What were you two talking about?" he asked. The question came less from a place of jealousy and more from a concern that she was jeopardizing his well-paying catering gig with her drunken conversations.

"Old movies," she managed to reply, supporting herself on the kitchen counter as the room began to descend into a slight spin.

"Oh Rons, you must be bored out of your mind. These academics are a snooze fest, but thankfully have money to burn on hors d'oeuvres."

"Yeah. Yawn," she lied, pushing a recently prepared salmon canapé into her mouth. "Actually, I think I'm going to go home."

Aaron looked disappointed for a moment and then smiled thankfully. "You do look tired."

"The dog needs to go out anyway."

"Well, thanks for coming with me, babe. You want me to call you a cab?"

"No, I want to walk a bit. Then I'll just hop on the streetcar."

Aaron wiped his hands on his apron and leaned over and gave her a kiss, hovering over a cheese platter ready to be brought out to the living room. When he pulled back he made a face. "Have you been drinking peach schnapps?"

Ronnie nodded.

"You know you really shouldn't be drinking. Just in case." He gently patted her belly, still speckled with cookie crumbs, and broke into a grin. "When can you take a test?"

She flinched, stepping back slightly. "Aaron, don't."

"But . . ."

"Don't. Not here."

"I'm sorry. Call me when you get home."

"I won't wait up."

"Take the cheese plate out with you while you leave."

Charlie loved his wife. He would go home to her that night and fall asleep next to the familiar comfort of her aging body, listening to her noisy sighs while he slipped in and out of vivid dreams of Ronnie—an Angela Vickers look-alike in a little black dress, a pale girl with the most piercingly beautiful laugh he'd ever managed to pull from someone with the minor wit he was able to muster.

He would never tell his wife about what happened at the party, about those dreams he had in their bed that night. Instead he slipped out of their bed and crept noiselessly past Noah's bedroom door and into the bathroom. He found his prescription sleeping pills, washed them down with tap water from his cupped palms, and only briefly wondered if it was unwise to mix them with drink. He returned to bed and lay staring at the ceiling, waiting for the pills' gentle wave to take him, hoping that he would sleep deeply enough to avoid further thoughts of Ronnie. But when his eyes opened and his whisky and peach schnapps hangover set in, her face was all he could think about.

The next day he called the party's host and found out that Ronnie was "no one. Just the caterer's girlfriend."

"Bit of a crush, Charles?" the party's host said good-naturedly.

"At my age you get your thrills where you can, I suppose."

"You know, we throw an entire party in your honour and you spend the night talking to the caterer's girlfriend. Typical Charles Stern."

"I don't know. I liked her. I found her relaxing."

"There's nothing wrong with wanting to be surrounded by beautiful things."

He asked for the caterer's contact information.

(CHAPTER THREE)

Ronnie was a slight girl. *A slip of a girl*, her mother would tell her. Slender and pale, like a fragile bird with a boisterous, bawdy laugh. She was one of those girls who was sick all through her childhood, who missed school repeatedly and was always in the midst of getting tests done for something or other. They never found anything concrete, but her mother would force-feed her protein drinks "to keep her weight up" and would constantly hover over her in fear that she would suddenly collapse or relapse.

Despite the fact that it was morbid, a doctor's office was where Ronnie always felt most at home. Even when she got older and stronger she would relish a trip to the doctor to fight an ear infection or get a tetanus shot. She longed for the coolness of crisp paper gowns and shiny stainless steel countertops, enjoyed the sterile order of glass jars full of cotton balls and wooden tongue depressors. Enjoyed the way the doctor would touch her in his cold, impersonal way.

Even though she was always sick, Ronnie grew to become reckless about her survival. In the face of her frailty, she had an optimism and vigour that poured out of her, flushing her cheeks, as if she might collapse from the sheer joy of being alive. A youth that teetered on the brink of supposed death gave her a fearlessness that most would never enjoy, and while those close to her were consumed with an anxiety about wellness, she had virtually no problem venturing into the world without the worry it would betray her. For these reasons it was natural she would wander over to Charlie at a party where she knew no one.

Charlie was the opposite—at his core he was resilient, robust, and ruddy, but hopelessly and helplessly neurotic. In perfect health, barely a case of the common cold to his name in the past decade, he obsessed over the various cancers he believed he was possibly and probably developing daily. Charlie was well travelled, experienced and educated, yet constantly terrified. Simple tasks like checking into a hotel, getting a haircut, or dining at restaurant were close to impossible for him thanks to his irrational fear. Spontaneity of any kind was completely out of the question. He was outwardly confident in a cocky, charming way, yet his swagger was peppered with a self-deprecating awkwardness that had allowed Ronnie to dominate the banter, allowed her to feel like she was in control. For these reasons it was natural he'd be charmed by Ronnie approaching him at a party where he knew everyone.

CHAPTER FOUR

Ronnie found out that Charlie was a writer a few days later. She was on a break from her shift at the hair salon, seated in a folding chair, absently watching that afternoon's hair appointments while eating the prosciutto and Gouda sandwich Aaron had made for her for lunch. While casually flipping through the weekly free paper with vague interest, there, on page sixty-two, was a picture of Charlie in the books section.

Charles W. Stern is an award-winning novelist, poet, and teacher. He lives in Toronto with his wife, Tamara Gardiner, and their son, Noah.

According to the paper, he was giving a talk that week at the university, an event sponsored by the faculty to celebrate his new position as writer-in-residence, starting in January. The date and time was printed below the photograph—a grainy black-and-white headshot that was obviously taken ten years previous, his round smiling face staring back at her from the page on her lap. Ronnie had never been to a talk by a poet before, never felt the desire to do so, but she took careful note of the date and time and considered what it would mean to see him again. Reasoned the interest was harmless.

Clutching the paper, Ronnie stared out into the mid-afternoon chaos of the salon: the flash of scissors, the hot roar of dryers, her co-workers stern-faced and clipping, or engaged in the same repetitive small talk every new client brought with them. She ran her finger over the shot of Charlie a few times, her fingertips blackening slightly from the ink, and then shut the paper abruptly. It should have occurred to her earlier that a poet might appear at a faculty Christmas party, might be the focus of interest for the other guests, but her concerns had been more focused on cookie crumbs and dress hems than his vocation.

She tried very hard not to romanticize this new detail, but it was close to impossible not to savour the fact that she had shared peach schnapps shots with a published writer. That she was the only one in that room of people that he had showed interest in. It simultaneously terrified and elated her.

Maybe, if she was lucky, he was unhappily married.

"Hey, Rons. Space cadet, wake up."

Lisa, a curvy and broad-shouldered fellow hairdresser with sleeve tattoos and dramatic makeup, suddenly called in her direction and broke her from her thoughts.

"Your two o'clock cut and dye is here. And if you're not done that sandwich, I'll eat it 'cause I know that wonderful boy of yours made it for you."

"Scavenger."

"Hey, I don't have anyone at home making me sandwiches, thanks very much. I take what I can get."

"Yeah, but you've got enough boys buying you dinner."

"Give me the fucking sandwich."

Ronnie smiled and offered the other half in her direction. "You're welcome to it."

Ronnie stood up, kicking clumps of cut hair from underfoot and brushing crumbs from her lap. As an afterthought she turned and reopened the paper to page sixty-two, carefully tearing out the picture of Charles W. Stern. She folded it twice into a tiny tight square and stuffed it into the billfold of her wallet.

"Man, this shit is delicious," Lisa said with her mouth full as Ronnie returned to work.

On Thursday evening Ronnie told Aaron she was running some errands and instead went to see Charlie read at the university. She sat quietly in the back of a theatre with what felt like endless rows of seating and watched as Charlie read a handful of poems and gave his talk on the creative process. She barely understood any of it, the poems or the creative process, and was embarrassed as she watched those around her nod in agreement or stand in single file at the microphone to ask him questions about his genius.

They would announce their credentials before they spoke, as if to prove to him that they were allowed to speak.

"My name is Emma, and I'm doing my master's in . . ."

"My name is Alan, and I have my Ph.D. in . . ."

"My name is Joyce, and I'm the author of . . ."

My name is Ronnie, and I cut hair.

She began to think coming had been a terrible idea. Without the confidence and buoyancy of a bottle of red wine and a little black dress, Ronnie felt like a stupid girl whose job it was to bring canapés on trays. She pulled on a frayed piece of wool from her blue cardigan and longed to retreat out the back door.

Onstage Charlie was a different man than the one she had met at the party—now confident, learned, his answers constructed of words Ronnie didn't know. Despite her insecurities, she was pleased to be in the same room as him, happy to know he still existed a week later, that she hadn't imagined him at that party.

When the talk was finished and the audience burst into a wave of applause, Ronnie was sure Charlie had spotted her at the back of the room. He paused ever so slightly, shifted his frame toward her, and seemed to squint in her direction, before his face relaxed into an expression of pleasure. He was escorted off to a table piled with books by a pretty blonde girl, barely twenty and likely a university volunteer, but instead of lining up or waiting for him to finish his signing and say hello, Ronnie pulled on her coat and left. When she was in the street in front of the venue she felt hot with the embarrassment that she had stalked him and was worried about what he would think. It didn't occur to her to be concerned that she had an urge to see him at all. That she had lied to Aaron about where she was.

On her way home from the event she picked up some dog food and milk from the convenience store, proof to show Aaron that she was engaging in something innocent and helpful. The items were unnecessary, given that Aaron barely looked up from his place on the couch when she wandered into the living room and said hello.

"How was your day?" he asked absently, flicking through channels until he settled on a predictable sitcom complete with canned laughter.

"Uneventful," she offered, nestling in beside him.

She lay her head in his lap, and while he ran his fingers through her hair, she thought of Charlie.

(CHAPTER FIVE)

CHARLIE

I write because it makes me feel interesting, wanted, desirable, wise. Because it's an itch that won't be scratched, but I just keep scratching and scratching until it bleeds, because that word was fifty cents and that one a dollar, this one two, and after this sentence is done I'll be able to buy a steak dinner.

I thought that being a writer would satiate me. I thought once I was the greatest, the beloved, the celebrated, the critically acclaimed, the itch would finally relent. But it never did cease, and as time passes I become more and more paralyzed by my own success. By my own failure that only I call failure. It's impossible to complain about success unless you're paying someone $175 an hour to listen (which I do, thank you very much). No one wants to hear how dismayed you are by the fact that everyone adores you. About how you feel like you're not doing enough to be adored. But I am dismayed. I live in a constant state of discomfort and dissatisfaction, amused by nothing and disappointed by everything.

This feeling? This quiet nagging voice inside my head that proves I'll never be satiated? This is where all the romance, all the "I'm a writer" bullshit goes to die.

What once was thrilling—a "craft," a "calling"—has become nothing more than an endless stream of tiny hotels and tiny towns, readings to a packed house and then readings where two people show up—one is a homeless man there for the snacks and the other is my publicist. Late nights spent away from home staring at the flashing cursor on a computer screen, paralyzed because nothing comes even though the questions of "how's it coming" never cease. Interviews and discussions and talks about "process" and young men who smell like cigarette smoke and too much sex asking me to mentor them, to read and critique their manuscripts about consuming lady flesh and doing blow. I listen to them talk about authors and ideologies, and I am keenly aware that there is a certain type of female that falls all over herself to grind her pelvis against their corduroy crotches. The kind of female who thinks a poem written about her is a gesture with meaning, when really it has even less depth than a porn pin-up pressed under a mattress.

I met Ronnie on a Friday evening in December at a university party at someone's too-huge-for-two-people Annex house. The kind of house where the books are shelved chronologically by genre and dusted by a maid service. A well-meaning professor friend of mine invited me in the hopes of impressing the faculty with my presence, and I just drained the host's expensive whisky offering, nodding my thank-yous at people who let me know they enjoyed my latest book.

"Oh, that's good, because I wrote it just for you," I longed to smarmily spit in their faces.

But you can't.

You have to be grateful.

Always grateful.

Always humble.

"Thank you. That means so much to me. It's an honour."

I don't imagine I impressed anyone.

I just drank more whisky and contemplated the diseases I could acquire from room-temperature decapod crustaceans prepared by imbeciles, and then Ronnie appeared. Tall and sleek and semi-clad, her hair so shiny, she walked across the room toward me in a little black dress—and she wouldn't have cared about books if I had begged her to. A girl like that doesn't care about books. A girl like that has a single shelf of mismatched volumes, gifts she's never read from friends she doesn't much like. One of the books is full of martini recipes and another is *Horton Hears a Who!* She reminded me of my irrelevance. She had no idea who I was in a room full of people who desperately needed to know me, people who threw empty compliments my way, female students who wanted to claim I had flirted with them, people so pleased that I would be the Massey College Writer-in-Residence in January, and who hoped I'd agree to attend their dinner parties. Judge their competitions. Mentor their sex-and-smoke-stinking faux poet children.

The next day my wife asked me why there was a shot glass in the pocket of the pants I'd left on the floor when I had gone to bed the night before. The only thing I could think to tell her was that I stole it. She just stared at me and shook her head.

I write because I don't have to be cautious when I do it. With my wife I have to be cautious. With my son I have to be cautious. When I write I can simply destroy everything I touch. While strangers think my life is incredibly thrilling, it's actually so completely fucking boring that I'm forced to write books about the things I really want to do. About the drama I want to create. About the girls I want to fuck. About this girl I want to fuck.

I knew I wouldn't have to be cautious with Ronnie. A girl like that doesn't want caution. She wants to be ripped from what is normal and predictable. A girl like that is reckless, and wanting, and so much more. A girl like that slips a shot glass in my pants pocket because it seems like the obvious thing to do. She doesn't care that I'm married, or famous or boring or anything at all.

It's not even that she wants to break things, it's that breaking things comes naturally to her.

My $175-an-hour therapist says I have dissatisfaction syndrome, although I am quite sure she made that up to continue her billing cycle. "You always want something different, Charlie, and you need to work on being satisfied with the things you've been given."

But why? But why? But why?

Apparently it means that I am destined to be unfulfilled, that I will always be searching for something more. A search that fills me with anxiety and a constant feeling of failure. A search that leads me to beautiful women at dinner parties.

I think I just found something more.

RONNIE

Charlie was the sweetest kind of sickness from the moment I met him. He was the secret thrill of possible infidelity embodied in a package of ridiculous awkwardness. Lately there hadn't been the secret thrill of infidelity—only Aaron and the predictable comfort of a love that refused to go wrong. Of course I had wanted, and of course there were moments after pints where a touch or a light kiss from a stranger or misguided friend promised something, but I didn't trust those promises the same way I trusted Charlie. Immediately. Without reason.

The nice thing about Charlie was that Aaron, who could have easily found his way into modelling underwear if he hadn't been so interested in gastronomy, would be incapable of becoming jealous of someone like Charlie. Not that Aaron was vain, just that Charlie was an unlikely suspect. Aaron knew he was beautiful and knew I was lucky to have him. In fact it often felt like everyone around us knew I was lucky to have Aaron, a subtle comment about my luck inserted here and there at dinner parties to ensure I felt sufficiently inferior to a wonderful man like Aaron.

I had never really disputed the fact that Aaron was better than me . . . it was one of those universal truths that everyone simply accepted. He had also been generous enough to take the time to fix me, because before him I was on good days careless and on bad days reckless. Aaron had made it a personal project to make me "better" and he was confident he was close to completing his task.

The fact that he trusted me to have his baby and not break it was proof of that.

I was lucky to have someone like Aaron take care of me, and because of that no one could be jealous or wary of someone like

Charlie—at least no one would ever be suspicious of someone like me spending time with someone like Charlie.

And despite my luck in Aaron being self-sacrificing enough to take someone like me on, I shoved that entire cookie in my mouth.

(CHAPTER SIX)

"Everything okay, honey?" Aaron called from the other side of the bathroom door.

Ronnie stood at the sink, staring down at the store-bought test, its single blue line stating what she knew already. She tossed it in the wastebasket.

"Yeah, I'm fine."

"Is there news?" Aaron was leaning against the other side of the locked door in anticipation.

"No news. I'll be down in a sec to help with dinner."

"Oh."

A pause. Neither of them moved, the reality of another negative test sinking in.

"I'll be down in a sec, okay?"

"Are you okay?" Aaron offered, despite the fact that he himself was clearly wounded.

"I said I was fine. What do you want to eat?"

"Honey, I'm sorry."

"Aaron, please."

"We can just reheat some leftovers. It's fine."

Ronnie and Aaron had been trying to have a baby for a few years. In reality, it was more an unspoken agreement that they wouldn't try *not* to have a baby. And, like most things in their lives, the fact that it wasn't working was also mostly unspoken. Additionally unspoken was the idea that the ill health of Ronnie's youth had left her insides unpredictable, though the doctors couldn't find any concrete reason why she couldn't conceive. Ronnie wasn't even sure she wanted a baby, but she knew that not being able to have one left her feeling like a failure. Aaron's constant lingering outside the locked bathroom door certainly did not help.

"You know, maybe it's time we talked to someone," Aaron called from the hallway. "People do it all the time, you know."

"I know they do. I just don't want to."

"But why? If it's going to help."

"I just don't want to. Not yet. Okay?" She listened to the sound of his feet finally padding off to the kitchen and exhaled a heavy sigh.

Despite the five years they had been together, Aaron and Ronnie had never bothered to get married. Aaron had always assumed that Ronnie was the type of girl who didn't care about white weddings and gift registries, and Ronnie assumed that Aaron would never ask. Because of this they had settled into a life that lazily assumed they would be together until death.

Ronnie washed her hands and splashed some water on her face before joining Aaron in the kitchen. He had a familiar look of concern on his face but said nothing, pulling a plastic-wrapped lasagne pan from the fridge and preheating the oven.

She generously put her hand on his shoulder, a gesture of reconciliation that he welcomed. "Listen. We'll try for a few more months and then I'll go, okay?"

Aaron smiled. "You sure?"

"Yes, but let's not talk about it until then, okay?"

"Okay. I promise." He turned and kissed her on the forehead, and then returned his attention to the lasagne pan.

Ronnie sat down at the kitchen table. Ramona, their hyperactive, rescued Rottweiler, ambled up to her and leaned against her knee, staring upwards with the expectation of a cookie. Ronnie thought about how they had moved into their two-bedroom first-floor apartment in Parkdale under the unspoken assumption that the second bedroom would one day be painted pink or blue or yellow. How as they had slept-walked into their late twenties, and then into their early thirties, breeding became a given, given that everyone else in their lives was doing it.

Aaron and Ronnie travelled in a circle of friends who lived their lives like they were collecting Monopoly cards. The baby card would complete the set. A natural progression that at first would come eventually and then would come immediately. No questions asked.

Ronnie was not entirely sure who had made this decision, it was simply one that had happened, that had been expected, and it didn't seem entirely negative, so she has been swept along with it without question.

Ronnie watched as Aaron began rummaging around in the fridge for the components of a salad. She staved off a sudden urge to cry, knowing that her disappointment was not connected to an inability to get pregnant but rather to her constant ability to disappoint, even when she was doing everything in her power not to.

I don't even know how to be a real woman. I can't make a casserole and I can't even breed.

Recently, during a routine examination, her doctor had found some wayward cells, tiny suspect growths that glowed white when her cervix was dosed with vinegar and lit up on the gynecologist's table. Ronnie was told it was nothing to be worried about, that it was "common for women to experience cervical changes." But the tests were scheduled and the biopsies performed, with bright-eyed med students mumbling covertly and thoughtfully pointing at the coloured blob on the television screen in the examination room. Ronnie clung to the word "routine" and stared at her endless stream of negative pregnancy tests and felt very little.

The occasional late-night Google search, fuelled by red wine and morbid curiosity, revealed that worry was something she was allowed to do if she really wanted to. She shared little news with Aaron, his interest in her body parts driven by pleasure and production rather than any vague indication of possible tragedy. Aaron was particularly good at convincing himself and those around him that there was nothing to be worried about, even when there was. Because of this Ronnie had learned to disregard him when judging the severity of the situation.

It was for this reason she would come to enjoy Charlie's ability to overreact to everything. As much as it irritated most of the people around him, his fear of catered food, his panic over misshapen moles and acid-reflux-as-heart-attack charmed her, made her feel like life was much more precarious and therefore valuable than Aaron's stoic nature suggested.

"Maybe it's stress," Aaron said, serving the reheated lasagne onto mismatched plates.

"What do I have to be stressed about?" she asked.

"Well, you seem a little absent lately. Somewhere else."

Ronnie poured herself a glass of Merlot and shook her head. She enjoyed drinking wine immediately after a pregnancy text.

"Really, Aaron, I'm fine. We'll just keep trying. These things take time. That's what everyone tells me," she said unconvincingly.

The truth was she was tired of the econo-box of pregnancy tests always under the bathroom sink, the strategic fucking at odd hours, and the hopeful looks from Aaron in those few days before her period. Every month he would ask if she was late with an embarrassing glee that made Ronnie slightly nauseated. It bothered her that he knew her cycle well after years of tracking it carefully and yet asked the question regardless. She had often contemplated going on the pill without telling him, but there seemed to be no point given how barren she now believed herself to be.

"It's okay, sweetie," Aaron offered, lightly putting his hand on Ronnie's arm. "Maybe next time. There's always next time."

During a five-minute conversation at a party in the Annex Ronnie suddenly became unsure about the blind path she was on. She was keenly aware that decisions had been made for her most of her life. By doctors and lovers and family. That she had failed to fight those decisions all the way to that two-bedroom apartment and that negative pregnancy test in the bathroom wastebasket.

And in the week since meeting Charlie she hadn't slept with Aaron once.

It wasn't that she no longer wanted a baby, it was that she wasn't really sure she wanted Aaron's baby.

"Really, Aaron. I told you. I'm fine."

(CHAPTER SEVEN)

The letter arrived in the mailbox of Ronnie and Aaron's Parkdale apartment a few days after the reading at the library. Soon it would be Christmas Eve, so Ronnie assumed it was another holiday card from a family member she'd never heard of, one of Aaron's many cousins, aunts, or uncles who were always calling and asking when the baby was coming or when they'd get an invite to the wedding.

It came in a creamy white envelope and in grand, looping handwriting was addressed to Veronica Kline, care of Aaron's catering company, Indulge Catering, a name Ronnie had always found amusing given it seemed Aaron had never indulged in anything in his life. An office address at the university, without a name, was printed in Helvetica on a white label in the corner.

It was bold for Charlie to send a letter to Ronnie and Aaron's shared apartment, and Veronica felt a surge of panic and guilt as she sat down at the kitchen table to read it.

Dear Veronica,

It was lovely to meet you the other evening. You owe me a cookie. Why don't you come by my fancy brand new office when I move in next month? Bring a bottle of peach schnapps.

Charles

P.S. I have just remembered that Montgomery Clift was gay and his relationship with Elizabeth Taylor . . . although deep and meaningful and lifelong . . . was platonic, so I have changed my mind about wanting to be him.

There was no phone number anywhere on the letter or envelope, a deliberate omission, she thought, for discretion and safety, meaning that she would have to take her chances and simply show up unannounced one day.

Ronnie glanced at the brand new kitten and puppy calendar affixed to the fridge with alphabet magnets and noted how many days it was until "next month."

When Aaron came home that evening she gave him a hug and a kiss as soon as he came through the door.

"What's with you?" he asked, smiling.

"Nothing. I just wanted to let you know I missed you," she lied.

(CHAPTER EIGHT)

The week between Christmas and the New Year was frantic. Suffocating. Claustrophobic.

Ronnie made three batches of shortbread cookies for her in-laws that they took a few bites of and pretended to like. Charlie had sugar cookies made for him. He ate all twenty-four in twenty-four hours. Tamara commented on how he'd gained weight that year. Charlie retaliated by commenting that Tamara had gained weight that year. Noah destroyed the gingerbread house on display in their living room with his fists and had to be wrestled away from it scream-ing. Ramona ate one of Aaron's two Cornish game hens, fresh from the oven and stolen from the kitchen counter, made for their quiet Christmas dinner at home. Aaron asked Ronnie to change out of what she was wearing and into something more "appropriate" before they went to his parents' house for a second, less quiet Christmas dinner. Ronnie called Aaron a jerk under her breath, which Aaron heard but pretended he didn't. Noah tore open over a dozen pres-ents until he got bored and abandoned them all for a drink coaster he refused to let go of. Tamara drank too much eggnog after Noah had gone to sleep and told Charlie he needed to support his family and "man up." Charlie drank too much Scotch after Noah had gone to sleep and told Tamara she didn't understand his needs. Tamara threw up too much eggnog and Charlie found the sound of her heaving in the bathroom oddly satisfying. Aaron ate too much turkey and fell asleep on the couch of his parents' house while Ronnie faced numerous questions from them about her failure to breed. To escape, Ronnie locked herself in the bathroom of Aaron's parents' house and re-read Charlie's letter three times. Charlie locked himself in the bathroom of his in-laws house and had a panic attack. Later, Noah locked himself in the same bathroom and started screaming while Charlie's father-in-law tried to jimmy the lock with a Bay card. When Noah didn't stop screaming, Charlie escaped quietly through the garage to go for a walk to think about Ronnie, smoking a joint he'd hidden in the billfold of his wallet. While Charlie was walking and thinking it snowed. After fifteen minutes Tamara called him on his cellphone while he was high in the middle of the suburbs in the snow and asked him where the fuck he was. He could hear Noah screaming in the background. Hearing her in-laws argue from just beyond the bathroom door, Ronnie folded up the letter and counted the days until "next month" over and over again in her head.

(CHAPTER NINE)

The day Charlie started his writer-in-residency at the University of Toronto he found that he was nervous in much the same way children were nervous before the first day of school.

Tamara made him a leftover ham sandwich in the kitchen, wrapping it carefully in wax paper before slipping it into a brown paper bag, an act that only made his fears seem all the more childish.

"Really, Charlie. You'll be fine. Do you want to play the worst-case scenario game? Like you do with your therapist?"

Her voice was soothing, but Charlie felt anxiety rise painfully within him as he gripped his coffee mug. He tried various techniques to assuage it, fending off a full-blown panic attack with feeble breath exercises and positive thoughts that were quickly stamped out by terror.

"Why did I agree to do this?" he asked Tamara weakly while she packed files into her bag. He sat down at the kitchen table and put his head in his hands.

"Because it's good for us," she said, kneeling on the linoleum in front of him. She kissed him softly, stood up, and then pulled him to his feet. "Now come on, you're going to be late."

Charlie had been given a small office space and a meagre stipend under the condition that he did the occasional talk and spent at least a portion of his afternoons greeting eager young faces, each of them hoping that their thinly veiled memoirs would one day become bestsellers. Upon the invitation, Charlie had resisted the idea completely, but Tamara had a way with guilt that made saying no impossible.

"It's a terrible fucking idea."

"It's money, Charlie," she had said, her eyes wide with the kind of pleasure that only came with past disappointment.

He loathed the idea of it, but yes, money—something he had failed at acquiring most of his life, more specifically during his marriage (which, to be fair, was most of his life), something that had been a mostly unsaid but occasionally poked at sore spot since Noah's illness consumed their lives.

"I'm not good with people," he objected as she tried to usher him out the front door.

"You're fine with people. You're the only one who doesn't think so. You just convince yourself you're not. You know you're supposed to try these things. That's how you get better at them," she responded. The comment was intended to be supportive, but could only be read as patronizing.

Tamara had been participating in this scenario most of their marriage. Charlie would be terrified of something mundane and Tamara would talk him into and through it. She was skilled at being the stereotypical writer's wife, relished it really.

"And it's good for your career. It'll give you the time to write and will raise your profile," she said optimistically.

Charlie loathed the word "profile."

He felt his profile was a constant, unending work in progress that rarely amounted to anything. He had published books to wide acclaim, but he was still relatively anonymous, able to walk down the street without being recognized by the general public. There was the occasional five-figure book prize or grant, and an annual three-figure royalty statement, and Tamara had sacrificed herself to a fifty-hour workweek as a result. Being beloved by critics and intelligent readers didn't automatically mean financial security or fame (in fact, generally the contrary), and hiring Amanda to take care of Noah, the special schools and therapists for him, were costly. Someone with a less-selfish demeanour would have to foot the bill. Charlie was too temperamental, neurotic, and unpredictable to sacrifice anything. It was also those characteristics that had consistently prevented him from holding down a day job.

Tamara held out the brown paper bag in front of him in a final effort to get him on his way. "Do you want me to write your name on the bag?" she asked, grinning.

"Stop it."

"You know you're just being silly."

"It's different for you. You love your job."

This was true, but Tamara was always too quick to mention that he got to lounge around and drink Merlot with writer-types while she worked through spreadsheets into the wee hours. Every time the furnace failed or the porch needed repair, she would sigh noisily and ask Charlie if he was "planning to take on something paid anytime soon." That meant teaching or ghost writing or something equally insufferable, and Charlie obliged until the bills were paid up.

Charlie dreaded the writer-in-residence position because he despised young people, with their dreams and aspirations and smooth cheeks like baby's asses. Their youth and vigour and sexual appetites left him feeling inadequate, impotent, and the notion of being around them enough to teach them anything was horrifying. Even the occasional crush bestowed upon him by a pretty young thing was certainly not enough for him to tolerate things.

The guilt that accompanied Tamara's snide remarks only increased when Veronica started to consume Charlie's thoughts. Despite the fact it had been a few weeks since he had seen her in the back of the room at his reading (since she had promptly run away from him before he could get close enough to smell her, touch her again), he had thoughts about her daily. He tried to burn an image of her into his memory from only those two brief moments. Enough time had passed that he had managed to fictionalize her completely—what she wore, how she spoke, what she did for a living, what she liked to eat, what music she liked, and of course, what she looked like naked. He would watch his wife sleep, gaze at the folds of flesh that came with age and that gathered around her chin and under her arms, and he would promise himself he would try to put Ronnie out of his thoughts, that he would not see her again, that his life was good and Ronnie would only cause problems. He promised himself it would go no further than his fingertips on the inside of her thigh at a crowded Christmas party.

The feel of the inside of that thigh had been something he had most certainly memorized. It was enough fodder to allow him to pleasure himself in the shower behind a locked door.

He reminded himself that he loved Tamara over and over again, while they ate meals together or went to parties together. Their life together was largely good, much better than most imagined, thanks to the struggle that was Noah's unpredictable mental state.

It was good. It was good enough.

And he would be good in return.

Tamara fixed the collar on Charlie's jacket and again kissed him softly on the mouth. "Now go. You're going to be late."

"Okay. I'll see you at dinner. Are we still having those godawful friends of yours over?"

"Indeed we are. Oh, and Charlie?"

"Yes, dear?"

"I'm really proud of you. You know that, don't you?"

Yes, Charlie knew that. But he was no longer sure that it mattered.

Noah had recently begun writing numbers on the backs of things with a blue ballpoint pen.

It had started with paper—receipts, coupons, five-dollar bills that he would find on countertops and in drawers.

The numbers always seemed random, pointless, meaningless. The doctor told Tamara and Charlie to expect randomness in his behaviour, that it was nothing to worry about. It was normal, or rather normal for abnormal.

They allowed it because, although annoying, it seemed relatively harmless. They allowed it because the doctors told them repeatedly, "You should go to the place where he lives instead of expecting him to come to you." Come to normal. The numbers, the organization, it seemed to settle him down. Scrawling numbers on everything prevented him from screaming. Seemed to solidify his need for order.

His debilitating need for order.

Charlie would come home and Amanda would apologize profusely.

"He wrote on your books today, Mr. Stern. The ones in your office. I'm sorry, but I know you asked me not to stop him," she said, exhausted.

"It's all right. I understand."

"He could only really reach the first three shelves, so I moved as many as I could. I tried to pick out the more valuable ones."

Charlie noted when he went to survey the damage that Amanda had not moved any of the books he himself had written, multiple copies of poetry collections littering the floor with Noah's childish scrawl all over them.

Over time the numbers got higher.

What started as one- and two-digit numbers written on the back of takeout menus and Canadian Tire money grew into four- and five-digit numbers written on the bottoms of mugs and the undersides of tables.

One day Charlie came home to find that Noah had written 387 on the back of the television with a Wite-Out pen he'd found in Tamara's desk drawer.

Then it was 586 on the cushion of the recliner in marker.

Around this time Tamara stopped inviting guests over. Although she was generally calm and flexible, given years of dealing with Charlie's neurosis, she was quite proud of domestic order and her ability to keep house. She loved Noah, but his ongoing defacing of their belongings was a source of embarrassment that caused her to move her monthly book club meeting elsewhere.

"Maybe we should put plastic on the furniture," she said to Charlie one night over dinner.

"Don't be absurd," he replied.

"I'm only looking for solutions. It's not absurd to want to find a solution."

"This is the way it is. We have to learn to accept it." Charlie enjoyed being the rational one for once, while Tamara gazed mournfully at their pristine beige microfibre sectional.

Another time Charlie awoke from a nap in front of the television to Noah carefully scrawling 869 on his thigh with a Sharpie.

From there it just got worse, and soon they discovered what he was actually doing was some mysterious form of cataloguing.

Their fat, aging, orange cat Mille sported a collar with the number 1227. The garage door opener became 1376. Charlie paid for meals with bills numbered 1456 and 1457.

It simply couldn't be stopped. When Charlie pulled the pen from Noah's hands he screamed and pounded his fists with such violence it was terrifying. Charlie no longer had the energy to care that his home was being defaced, no longer cared about the questions and stares of potential dinner guests.

The doctor always said it would pass, like all his other phases, and that he would move on, but on a Monday afternoon Charlie came home from the university to find that Noah had begun the elaborate task of putting everything in the house in chronological order.

Again Amanda was exhausted and apologetic, panting at the doorway with hair dishevelled, her eyeliner smeared onto her temple.

"I'm so sorry, Mr. Stern, I couldn't stop him. He just got so upset—"

"It's okay, Amanda. I know whatever it is it's not your fault."

Sometimes it amazed Charlie that Amanda had not yet quit. He was constantly impressed with her resilience and tolerance, both of Noah and himself.

Charlie hung his coat on a hook in the hallway and braced himself for what he would see inside. Amanda readied herself for his reaction, placing her hand over her mouth as if to muffle a cry.

Sitting there, among spoons and empty plastic bottles, Tamara's suit jacket and the toaster oven, Noah looked up at Charlie and pointed to a small, clear space on the floor of the living room.

A space between the ficus plant, 868, and the vacuum, 870.

"Daddy. 869."

(CHAPTER TEN)

RONNIE

I hate mangoes. Mostly because they're all work and no pay off.

Aaron has that kind of patience and I have none. I watch him cut it open in the most economical way possible—peeling so perfectly that no piece of flesh is spared. It's methodical, with no sensuality in an easily sensual act. No rebellious sticky sweetness dripping the length of his arm, no juice licked from fingertips. Just evenly carved segments lined up on a plate, his hands scrubbed antiseptically clean of any evidence of the endeavour.

That piece of fruit could be a metaphor for all of it; he peels it, cautiously, carefully, and I eat it. Consume it. He does all the work and I enjoy the results.

I have never been the kind of girl to invest, never wanted to take the time. I always want it quickly, and now. Fuck hardboiled eggs, fuck soufflés, fuck five-year terms and two-year leases, sometimes even fuck microwave burritos.

I'm the kind of girl who wants to reach my hand into a cereal box and shove a fistful of Shreddies into my mouth. I never really understood what was wrong with that. Sometimes you just want to shove a fistful of Shreddies into your mouth and have no one give you shit about it, especially not the person who eats in your kitchen and sleeps in your bed and walks your dog. The same person who knows how to patiently peel a mango, and balance a chequebook, and what prime is right now.

Aaron and I will be stuck in traffic in our twenty-year-old Volvo station wagon and I'll be singing along with the radio, eating potato chips, like we're on a road trip, when really we're just going to his mom's house for roast beef, then he'll change the station to catch the traffic report and tell me not to get chip crumbs on the upholstery.

He does all the work and I eat cereal straight from the box, drink milk from the carton, and steal that last slice of mango.

He cleans up all my messes.

CHAPTER ELEVEN

At four in the afternoon on a Wednesday in the third week of January, Charlie was in a meeting with a nineteen-year-old undergrad about her 400-page opus on the transience of love. Nineteen-year-old undergrads were always writing novels about love, and Charlie was always forced to talk to them about it. Forced to lie and say he would show his agent. Forced to tell them they had "so much promise" and that they should "keep writing," even though he thought they should look into other career choices.

This particular undergrad was pretty—unkempt and unshowered, and perhaps slightly high, but certainly pretty—and he was willing to suffer through her endless ramblings on Neruda and Winterson to fulfill the office hour requirement of his residence. If he was honest, the office made him feel powerful, less like the stuttering, clumsy fool he believed himself to be, and more like the charming writer he hoped people saw.

He had just managed to tune this particular student out while inserting the requisite uh-huhs and yeses, when there was a knock at his office door. Without rising from his chair, he called out an invitation to come in and watched the heavy wooden door slowly creak open.

Ronnie's flushed face appeared from behind it. Her hair was damp, and a heavy wool coat was pulled up to her chin. Charlie rose to his feet and maintained his composure.

"Hi Mr.—Charlie."

"Mr. Charlie?"

The nineteen-year-old undergrad shifted uncomfortably in her seat. Charlie was quite certain if he could get close enough to her she would have smelled incapable of using the residence coin laundry.

"Shannon, I'm sorry we'll have to cut this short today as my next appointment has just shown up," he said, gesturing toward Ronnie, who smiled in acknowledgement of his lie. "I'm very pleased with how your edits are coming along. You'll be close to publication soon."

Shannon, despite being stoned, knew the woman at the door was too old to be Charlie's next appointment. She started giggling.

"Thanks—*Mr. Charlie*," she finally said, smiling coyly—as coyly as a girl with dirty hair could smile.

She collected her belongings haphazardly, a pile of removed sweaters and various bags that she hung from her available limbs, and shuffled like a bag lady out the door. Ronnie moved out of her way but avoided eye contact as she closed the door behind her.

"Close to publication? Wow," Ronnie remarked genuinely, sitting in the chair that the undergrad had vacated.

"Not a chance. I always say that. It just means I get to spend less time with them."

"How awful."

"More awful than destroying their dreams?"

"I suppose not."

Ronnie crossed and then uncrossed her legs, scanning the room slowly. Books were piled haphazardly on every available surface, pushed up against walls, lying open face down on his desk. The room had the smell of damp paper.

"Your office. It's nice," she said.

"You're being kind."

"No. It's homey."

"Well I've been trying to keep it tidy. Just in case."

He was charming. Not bumbling. He was making Ronnie smile. A smile that didn't come from a place of mockery.

"Are all these books yours?" she asked.

"Yes."

"Have you read them all?"

"Most of them, yes."

"I don't read that much," she said, blushing.

"Reading's overrated."

She shifted her weight and absently picked up a collection of Auden's poetry from his desk and flipped through it.

"Well Miss Kline, it took you a while to get here," Charlie said, changing the subject.

"A month, yes. I've been busy."

"Busy not reading?" he laughed.

"Just busy."

This was actually not true. She had certainly not been busy, and she had actually been to his office much earlier than that but felt foolish when she learned that he had not moved in yet. A hairdresser was not aware that the university was still closed for the holiday break. She didn't mention this to Charlie, hoping that the distance between the party date and now would make her seem desirably casual about the visit. Desirable in general.

"I take it you got my letter?"

"No, I just followed the smell of desperation."

"Cute. And did you bring the schnapps?"

"Yes, indeed I did. And two bologna sandwiches just in case you were hungry. I figured you'd like them given that mustard stain on your shirt the night of the party."

"Very observant of you. Maybe you've got writer in you somewhere."

"Doubtful." Ronnie laughed nervously, returning the Auden to his desk to reach into her bag. She retrieved a silver flask and a plastic-wrapped kaiser roll, passing them both across his desk. It struck Charlie that a bologna sandwich was the perfect thing for a girl like Ronnie to bring. He felt comfortable, like she wasn't intimidating him. He was buoyed with confidence.

"Did you enjoy the reading the other night?" The words struck Ronnie suddenly, and she felt her stomach burn and knot with embarrassment.

"What reading?"

"My reading that you came to and ran away from before saying hello?"

"Oh, that reading," she said, trying to be casual. "I didn't really understand it but you seemed like you knew what you were talking about."

Charlie laughed as he unscrewed the cap of the flask. He took a swig, grimacing when the syrupy sweetness hit his lips.

"Honey, I never know what I'm talking about. God, how can you drink this?" He eyed the flask suspiciously. "Who's Aaron?"

"Excuse me?"

"Aaron. The flask. Engraved," he said, holding it up and toward her. "*Sweet Rons, all my love, Aaron.*"

"You know full well who Aaron is," Ronnie said combatively. "You sent mail to his business address."

"Business address? You mean your apartment where the two of you live together, right?"

"How do you know that?"

"It's not hard to get people to tell me things, Ronnie."

"Speaking of people telling me things, how's your sick child, Charlie?"

"I told you he's not sick. He has autism."

"I hear that takes a lot of work. You must be a devoted parent."

The accusations hung in the air. They'd transformed the conversation from playful to combative in mere seconds, gotten off to a bad start, despite the schnapps and sandwiches.

"Okay. Glad we got that out of the way. You're married with a special needs kid, and I'm living with someone. Yet, I still came to your office, didn't I?"

"Just because people have the things in their lives that they're supposed to want doesn't mean that they're happy, despite what other people may think," Charlie said, punctuating his convoluted wisdom with another swig from the flask engraved with Aaron's name.

"Sounds like you're already drunk."

"No, but I'd welcome it."

Charlie took another swing and then put a framed picture of his family face down on his cluttered desk with no attempt to hide the gesture from Ronnie.

"Are we going to have an affair?" he asked her nonchalantly, unwrapping his sandwich and then licking the leaking mustard from his fingers.

"What kind of question is that?"

"A relatively simple one; are we going to have an affair?"

"Well, I'm not really sure yet."

"You've had some time to think about it."

Ronnie paused for a moment, looked at him thoughtfully, her expression betraying little. She noticed that Charlie had managed to get mustard on his shirt. Again. "You've got some . . ."

"So, Ronnie, what will make you sure?"

"Your shirt . . ."

"Never mind that."

"Finish your sandwich. It's a little too early for that kind of talk."

Charlie laughed. "Too early in the day, or too early in our relationship?"

"Now we have a relationship? I told you. Finish your sandwich."

"Aaron didn't make it, did he?"

"Of course Aaron didn't make it. Aaron doesn't make bologna sandwiches. And Aaron doesn't know I'm here. I don't know why I'm here."

"Take a guess."

Ronnie paused for a moment, picking at her sandwich longingly, pulling pieces of the stale white bread bun apart with her fingers. "You're provoking me, Charlie."

"I figure given our circumstances, we might as well get everything out on the table, no?"

"I don't know. I guess I can't stop thinking about you. We spoke for five minutes but I can't stop thinking about you," she said. She returned to the Auden, if only to busy herself with something while tolerating his questions.

"Well, it seems you do have some willpower. It took you over a month to get here."

"I was at the salon on a break. I saw your picture in the paper."

"I'm always in the paper."

"I'm always at the salon."

"So you saw my picture in the paper."

"And I decided it would be harmless."

"So far, entirely harmless."

"It doesn't feel harmless."

"Put down the book, Ronnie."

"Because of your son."

"My son's name is Noah. He's eight."

"I was a sick child."

"Again. He's not that kind of sick, " Charlie sighed, looking frustrated. "Put down the book, Ronnie."

Despite the initial awkwardness, the shame in flirting shamelessly with a married man, a father, she felt a closeness to Charlie upon hearing about Noah. It seemed strange to want a married man more because he had a child, more attachments, more reasons to stay, but she felt an immediate closeness that warmed her completely. Because she had been sick herself she wanted to tell him that she had loved her youth, regardless of the constant trips to the doctor and the endless poking and prodding. Children adapt, she wanted to tell him. Children can find beauty in a hospital room, while the rest of us are compelled to suffer and complain over hangnails and disabled Internet connections. Children love things that love them back.

She wanted to ask Charlie what it was like to have that kind of love in his life, because she was quite sure she would never have it herself.

She finally obliged in returning the book to the desk. "I know, I just meant I was sick and I turned out okay."

"More than okay, really."

"Do you think we're going to have an affair, Charlie?"

"Maybe we should go for a walk first."

It was snowing movie-style snow as they walked through campus, big fat flakes that caught in Ronnie's lashes and melted on her lips, and again she pulled her navy wool peacoat high around her neck, shivering.

"Cold?" Charlie asked, putting his arm around her, the first time he had touched her since his fingers met the inside of her thigh at the party weeks ago. Her stomach twisted and dipped, sending a shiver through her that she concealed with the cold. She was amazed a man so awkward came so easily to touching her. She leaned into him ever so slightly, testing the weight of his body, testing how much he could hold of her before things fell apart. With his free hand he pushed his glasses up his nose awkwardly.

"I'm really glad you came to my office, Ronnie."

It had just begun to get dark, the red and green Christmas lights strung across campus bursting with a sudden blink of light. She welcomed the darkness, wary that someone might see them.

"So what do you do? At the salon."

"What most people do at salons. I'm a hairdresser. I work on Yonge Street."

"Do you like it?"

"Enough. It's busy. What do you do? I mean, besides write poems, talk about the creative process, and tell writers they're ready for publication soon."

"I don't do much of anything else, really. I write things and people buy them occasionally."

"What does your wife do?"

"Why would you ask me that? Right away?"

"Well, you know that Aaron is a caterer, it only seems fair, really."

"Yes. Fair. Tamara is an environmental consultant for one of those companies that destroy the environment."

"Seems valiant."

"More well-meaning than valiant. She makes most of our money, just in case you were wondering how a poet can be such a snappy dresser. And she travels a lot."

Charlie was unsure why he added that last detail. Or maybe he knew exactly why he added it.

"Who takes care of your son when you're both working?"

"We hired someone. Amanda. Someone who understands his—"

"Special needs."

"I always hated that term. We all have special needs. To say it's just people like my son who have them is ridiculous. His needs are easier than most."

Ronnie nodded in agreement, as if she understood even though she probably didn't. "Does Amanda live with you?"

"Sometimes. She has a room in our house but she's at her boyfriend's house a lot in the evenings. When we're home."

"Is Amanda pretty?"

"Why?"

"I'm trying to picture her."

"Yes. She's pretty. Blonde. Cheerful. Kind. But not particularly interesting."

"I assume a lot of people don't seem interesting to you."

"That's not true."

"Does she read books?"

"I suppose, yes. She reads books. Most people read books."

"Have you ever fantasized about her?"

"God. Why do you ask questions like that?" he said, pretending
not to be pleased.

"You're saying that like you know what kind of questions I ask."

"I don't know. You seem . . . reckless. Like you enjoy sticking your finger in a wound or putting your hand in a fire."

Charlie saying this, out loud, seemed to solidify to the both of them that he didn't mind that Ronnie seemed reckless. In fact, her recklessness was just what he wanted.

"I like to take some risks, yes. That's true. Less now than I used to, of course," Ronnie said, smiling.

"Not me."

"I gathered that."

"From what?"

"Beige shirt."

"Shut up." He pushed her, playfully, but she tripped on her own boot and fell clumsily sideways into the snow. He laughed while apologizing, extending his arm toward her. She looked at it and up at him with a serious expression, her cheeks flushed with pink from the cold.

"Oh Ronnie, I'm sorry," Charlie said sincerely.

Ronnie took his hand tentatively and then suddenly, aggressively, pulled Charlie forward into the snow with her. He collapsed on top of her and then rolled sideways, laughing, until they were both lying on their backs, covered in snow. They turned their heads to face each other, a sudden moment of stillness overtaking them after a fit of laughter.

"Charlie, do you love your wife?"

A pause.

"Of course I do."

"Really?"

"We met each other very young. We were in our twenties. Still in university. And then we had Noah and he was—"

"But Noah's only eight?"

"Yes. He is."

Ronnie did the math in her head.

"So you had him when the two of you weren't happy?"

"Yeah. He was an . . ."

"Oh god. You don't have to say it."

"It's okay. He was an accident. Things weren't going so well between us at the time. But we were married and married people have children. They don't have . . ."

"You don't have to say that either. You had to have him. And you couldn't leave each other."

"I suppose the plan, however unspoken, had been to stay together until he was old enough. Until it was easier. But then he was diagnosed—"

"And it never got easier."

"But I don't regret it at all. He's the only bright spot in my life."

"I'm sure that's not true. You seem to have a lot of bright spots."

Charlie sat up and looked back at Ronnie in the snow, her expression soft as the flakes fell and then melted on her warm cheeks. He sighed quietly at the sight of her there, so calm, a place of solace in an otherwise anxious world.

"Ronnie—"

"No, Charlie. Not here. Not yet."

Instead he offered his hand and together they rose to their feet and stepped back onto the path.

Charlie was carefully gauging Ronnie's reaction to him divulging the precarious state of his marriage. Her face was relaxed, waiting on his next word without pressure.

Perhaps it was easier to tell things to strangers. Tell things to people who didn't expect anything from him. "I love her, Ronnie. It's just so—"

"—normal?"

"Yeah. That."

"I get it. I live normal every day. I live the kind of normal life that all my friends are jealous of."

"I'm enjoying the way you keep finishing my sentences."

"Sorry. Nasty habit."

"No, it makes me feel like we're—the same in some ways."

"I feel like in some ways I'm living your life."

"I think you're being generous. Or deluded."

"Maybe I'm here so I can help you live your life better?"

"So serendipitous that we met then. Strangers taking a walk in the snow. Talking about affairs."

"Hey. I never said anything about an affair."

"I think you did, actually."

Charlie's arm found a place around her waist.

CHAPTER TWELVE

"Are you working on a new project?" Tamara asked Charlie over chicken cordon bleu one snowed-in evening in February.

Animals cooked within other animals were always something Charlie had a hard time accepting. He'd once heard of something called a "Turducken," a high achievement of American gluttony in which a chicken is cooked inside a duck inside a turkey. The things that humans were capable of doing to themselves via food terrified him, but cooking was not his strong suit, and Tamara did the majority of it when Amanda wasn't around, just like she did the majority of almost everything else, so he rarely complained.

Noah was noisily tapping his fork on his plate in a methodical way and humming to himself. After many years of this kind of behaviour they had mostly learned to tune him out when it was necessary.

"Why do you ask?" Charlie gently put his hand on Noah's arm to cease the tapping. Noah let out a frustrated squeal, dropped his fork, and moved on to pounding the table with his fist.

"Just because you've been coming home late a lot. You seem to come home late only when you're working on a new project."

A new project, Charlie repeated in his head.

He was surprised by how liberally the lies suddenly flowed between bites.

"I've been taking notes for a new novel. A love story. About a girl. A really normal girl. A hairdresser. She's nothing special."

"Nothing special? Not to be rude, but why would anyone want to read a book about nothing special?" she said with her mouth full.

Tamara had always been Charlie's first reader, so he had come to expect her to be ruthless with her commentary. He encouraged it, as she was always right and never had steered him wrong with an edit.

"That's just it. She's special in her not-specialness."

"Not-specialness?" Tamara laughed and spooned more potatoes onto her plate. She was making fun of him, ever so slightly. He wanted to retaliate by telling her she should watch her second helpings, watch her waistline as it spread with each passing year. But of course he did not.

"Everything in our culture is about being special, unique, different and standing out. Maybe not special is the new special," Charlie realized how ridiculous it sounded as soon as it came out of his mouth.

"So who is she in love with?"

"Sorry?" Charlie coughed suddenly as the word caught in his throat.

"You said it was a love story."

"She's in love with someone special. Someone that the world thinks is special."

"Of course. A writer I assume?" She was grinning knowingly, almost mockingly, a small piece of spinach lodged between her teeth.

"It's early yet. In the process. I'm just outlining."

"You can be so predictable, Charlie."

"So supportive."

"I'm sorry. Really, that's wonderful, sweetheart. You haven't written a novel for a while."

Noah suddenly flung his fork violently across the kitchen. Tamara trailed after it, not wavering from the conversation.

"Will it be written from her point of view?"

"Now that you mention it, yeah. I think it probably will be."

Charlie considered this idea while Tamara returned to her seat and gave Noah back his fork.

What was Ronnie's point of view?

What did she think about when she was folding Aaron's laundry?

What do simple girls think about when they can't think in poetry? When they don't think in narratives?

Do they think about beaches and quiches and trips to the dentist?

Do they think about boys they meet on the subway and kiss in bars after a few too many rum and Cokes?

Do they think about something better?

Does a girl like Ronnie think about Charlie?

"When will it be ready for me to read?" Tamara asked.

Tamara was, above all things, a devoted reader, and he valued her reaction to his work above that of all others, handing her pages early in the process, while they were too naked for even Charlie to tolerate them. As a result she'd be thanked in countless acknowledgment pages since he began writing.

To Tamara I owe everything.
Tamara is the only reason I write.
Tamara, my first reader, my partner, my life.

Lies. Carefully constructed. Public persona. *Profile.*

He'd written so many variations on this sentiment that it had come to lose meaning. They were for all those middle-aged book club ladies, the ones who came to his readings, who asked him to sign their names in his books. Those women who felt safe because he was married but fantasized about him kissing them long and deep, his fingers creeping into the wetness between their thighs. A writer. A man who wrote love poems to blot out the monotony of their mediocre minivan lives.

The world had been told enough times that Charlie would be nothing without Tamara. In fact, he had made a point to publically emphasize his own pointlessness without her to lean on.

If he was honest, he didn't think he wanted her to read this one.

"I'm not sure just yet. I'll let you know."

"Well, I'm really proud of you, honey. It sounds like it will be a good one."

(CHAPTER THIRTEEN)

Sunday morning Ronnie lay in bed and, while staring at the ceiling, pondered very seriously whether fidelity was in the mind, in the mouth, or in the heart.

She could hear Aaron wandering through the apartment, jangling keys and neatly packing his backpack, oblivious to her deep considerations on the nature of commitment.

"Hey, Rons. I'm going to the gym, you sure you don't want to come with me?" he called from the kitchen.

Ronnie rolled her eyes dramatically in the dim morning light of their bedroom, Ramona curled up against her in a cocoon of blankets and pillows. She knew he had asked the question in full knowledge that she would never say yes, despite how he prodded her endlessly to get a membership. Ronnie hadn't physically exerted herself in any way other than running to catch a bus in years.

"No. I'm good. Thanks. Have fun," she responded, concealing her disdain.

"It might be good for you, considering."

"Considering what?" she spat.

"Well, you've been . . ."

"I've been what?"

"I'm just saying the gym can be good for your mental health. That's all."

Ronnie knew he meant that she was distant. She felt a pang of concern that he had noted her withdrawing silence, her new habit of staring off into space when they were together.

When she didn't respond he offered a question. "Are you planning to sleep all day?"

Aaron always asked these kinds of questions, and Ronnie loathed answering them. "What did you say? I can't hear you from here," she lied.

He came to the bedroom door with his coat and backpack on, not pressing on the issue of her ten previous hours in bed.

"When did you say your next doctor's appointment was?" he asked.

The question caught her by surprise. "A few weeks. Why?"

"I want to come," he said.

He looked awkward standing there, attempting to show his concern. It wasn't that he didn't care, of course, only that expressing sympathy didn't come naturally to him. Ronnie often excused it via his stifled upbringing.

"You don't have to do that. I'll be fine. They say it's routine. Just a follow-up."

"I know, but I still want to be there."

She wondered if he had sensed her absence and was trying to pull her back by showing increased worry over things he was generally stoic about.

"Really, it's no big deal."

"I know, Ronnie, but I said I want to be there," he snapped. "I feel like as soon as we get these abnormalities out of the way the sooner we can get back to our plan."

Abnormalities. The word and its lack of feeling hit her hard. The notion that her illness was an obstacle to breeding, nothing more.

Ronnie forced a smile despite the sting. "That would be nice. If you came."

"It's settled then. You sure you don't want to come to the gym?"

Ronnie shook her head.

Aaron left the house and Ronnie continued to ponder if bodies being exchanged were worse than thoughts being obsessed over. If all this innocent touching and fantasizing was really as wrong as it seemed.

If it was wrong at all.

If she could keep this thing with Charlie all in neat little private thoughts, then maybe it wasn't all that bad.

Was it really wrong to find solace in someone else when you felt so neglected? Was the betrayal really hers or was it Aaron's? He had made a promise to her that he would love her, give her what she needed, and now she found only emptiness, a nagging doubt that there must be more to love than this.

It was difficult not to list the things that Aaron did that drove Ronnie crazy, things she assumed Charlie would never even conceive of doing.

He washed his jeans inside out so they wouldn't fade, and hung them to dry in neat rows from their shower rod. He made her use a coaster, heaving a tremendous sigh when she failed to remember to do so. He hated that she ate the olives out of his martini with her fingers, cocking an eyebrow of judgment while she licked the gin from her fingertips. All those nagging questions he had about her sleeping too late and not going to the gym. The silent judgment as he collected her discarded clothes from their bedroom floor.

And the baby. All those relentless questions about the baby.

And while wisdom, or tradition, suggested that if she was so unhappy she should leave, there was a part of her that believed that holding together their lives with those private thoughts of Charlie, keeping a tolerable stasis that avoided any pain, was actually more generous than blowing the whole thing . . . his family, her life with Aaron . . . apart.

So while Aaron was at the gym she lay on her back in their bed, staring at the ceiling, and slipped her hand slowly into the front of her underwear, closed her eyes, and thought of Charlie.

(CHAPTER FOURTEEN)

The Chronology of Infidelity

A slow slide. A stumble you don't know how you made.

First there was just talking. Nothing more.
Just talking.
A shot glass in the pocket.
Then sharing secrets.
"I've never told anyone this."
Emotional infidelity. That's what they call it.
Drinking too many beers and kissing at last call.
Drinking too many beers and having phone sex.
"We can just make out."
The fucking.
The lying.

Falling in love. (Just don't fall in love.)
I love you I love you I love you
In love and planning an escape.
No other love that is happening to you right now is this big.

(CHAPTER FIFTEEN)

In the first few weeks after their walk in the snow Charlie and
Ronnie did innocuous, non-threatening things together.

There was just talking. Nothing more.

"You have the most beautiful neck, you know."

"You like my neck?"

"I like your neck."

Ronnie instinctually put her fingers on either side of her neck
and looked away shyly.

"It's a lovely neck."

"Do you have a neck thing?"

"A neck thing?"

"Some people have a breast thing or a foot thing. Maybe you
have a neck thing."

"Not as a rule. In fact, I think it may just be yours. My one and
only neck."

I just picture my hand on it. Drawing you to me. Kissing the length of it.

"In case it seems like I'm dense or unobservant, it's not just your
neck that's lovely."

"Not just my neck?"

Fishing.

"No. Not just your neck."

"What else is lovely, then?"

"Other parts. But it's easier to openly adore your neck than other parts of you."

"I feel like my neck might unfairly be the front runner. Given its constant exposure."

"You occasionally wear scarves. It's not as if you're exploiting it. It's a very demure neck."

In the absurdity of their conversations, Ronnie reasoned that there couldn't be anything wrong with feeling this light, nervous, and happy about a new companion.

We're just talking, she thought.

They engaged in activities they could easily justify, despite the fact they never told anyone they were spending time together. They would go for an afternoon coffee when Ronnie was finished her shift at the salon and when Charlie could take a break from his required time at the university. They sat across from each other awkwardly, Charlie responsible for bad jokes, and Ronnie responsible for inappropriate, teasing comments.

"Do you ever worry that people only like you because you're a famous writer?" she asked one afternoon.

"Famous is generous."

"Well, those people at that party all seemed to think you were important."

"Well, do you worry that people only like you because you're a hairdresser?"

She laughed. "Sometimes, I guess. People tell me really personal things and I'm never sure why."

"People don't tell me things, and I'm sure it's because they think I'll steal them."

"And sell them out."

"Precisely."

"Well, do you?"

"All the time. I'm surprised anyone talks to me, really."

"If I was you, I'd worry about false friends a lot of the time."

"That's funny. I never really worry that people like me at all. I can be insufferable."

"Tamara fell in love with you, though. She must have thought you were at least vaguely tolerable."

"Tamara never had very good taste in men."

"I think you're resigned to being hard on yourself, Charlie. I think it's lazy."

"Do you now?"

"Like you're living some easy cliché. I think acting like you're likable might actually suit you if you gave it a try."

Charlie enjoyed this suggestion. It certainly wasn't one that he, or anyone else, had thought of.

Ronnie and Charlie pretended to be friends, but every so often Charlie would hold a door open or put his palm lightly on the small of Ronnie's back, or Ronnie would lightly touch Charlie's arm at the elbow when laughing at his jokes.

Additionally, Ronnie found herself putting effort into her appearance that she hadn't since she and Aaron had started dating five years earlier. She'd make sure her bra matched her underwear and that her legs were shaved. She'd reapply lip gloss constantly and every so often excuse herself to the bathroom to check her teeth or smooth her hair.

This shift made her feel giddy, like a teenager, and she enjoyed the resulting self-conscious compliments that Charlie would inevitably pour all over her. He enjoyed that she was making an effort—he could barely remember the last time a woman had done that for him.

When they weren't together they would email each other, Charlie from his office at the university and Ronnie from the kitchen table at home while Aaron cooked complex dinners and talked about himself. As time passed they would fill each other's inboxes with hundreds, thousands of messages, meaningless and meaningful digital notes throughout the day that sketched out a picture of their lives. It was in this way that they were rarely apart, every moment of every day captured and shared.

What are you doing?
Nothing much. How are you?
I miss you.
That's sweet.
You're sweet.
When can I see you again?
As soon as possible I hope.
Do you miss me?
More than anything.

(CHAPTER SIXTEEN)

"It doesn't exactly take a genius to see that you've got something on your mind, girl," Lisa observed, shivering in the cold outside the salon's back door.

"I'm just tired," Ronnie said, watching Lisa smoke and wondering why she'd agreed to come outside to do so. The two of them huddled together against the wall in the alley, thankful for the break but lamenting the weather.

"Don't lie to me, Rons. Tired is the excuse people use when everything is shit and they don't want to talk about it."

"Fine. I've got something on my mind."

"Let me guess: is it your cervix?"

"Lisa."

Befriending Lisa meant a constant experiment in tolerance of the inappropriate. Ronnie wrapped her sweater more tightly around her and looked away uncomfortably.

"I told you, honey. It's not something you should be worried about. This kind of shit happens to women all the time. Abnormal results are our cross to bear. I'm sure it'll clear up."

"It's not that."

"Existential, then?"

Not entirely sure what Lisa meant, Ronnie nodded regardless. "Can you hurry up and finish that? It's freezing," she said, eager to change the subject.

Lisa ignored her and continued smoking. "You know, you're not obliged to do anything you don't want to. And you're not obliged to not do anything you want to."

"I don't know what you mean."

Ronnie knew exactly what she meant.

Lisa didn't push it. Simply flicked her cigarette in a slush puddle and pulled open the heavy metal door back to the busy salon.

CHAPTER SEVENTEEN

"My mother? She was obsessed. But sometimes I think she enjoyed it," Ronnie said. "The attention she got from doctors. From the other mothers. Attention she didn't get from my dad."

Ronnie was unpacking her life history during one of their coffee dates, dates that now happened at least three times a week, telling Charlie stories about what it was like for her growing up. He was enthralled with tales of her divorced parents and her subsequently emotionally damaged mother.

"Didn't that seem strange to you?" Charlie asked.

"I was a kid. Nothing seems strange when you're a kid. Only adults take the time to figure out that things are not right."

It was impossible for Charlie not to think of Noah, that perhaps the only thing wrong with him was how others perceived him.

"And anyway, it was good for me," Ronnie continued.

"How?"

"Well, I was doted on. I could do no wrong. And my absent father made every payment and bought every gift on time. Sure, my mother's anxiety made her enjoy her Chardonnay too much, but she was a really good mother."

"So rare that someone refers to their drunk mother as a good mother."

"She did her best," she said. "And I was useful. I gave her something to fix."

"Sounds familiar," Charlie offered.

"Your parents?"

"No. I meant Tamara. I'm her broken thing."

"You keep saying that."

"Well, to be fair, when Tamara met me I wasn't exactly functional."

"No?"

"I was a little boy masquerading as a badass," Charlie said, looking away, embarrassed.

"Well, some people like to have someone to take care of, I guess."

"It's funny, because as soon as we met it was a given we were going to be a couple. It was never questioned."

Ronnie chose not to pursue this. Talking about Tamara made her uncomfortable, despite the fact that she was endlessly curious.

"So. Are you going to sell me out, Charlie?"

"You mean for literature? Unlikely. I prefer having a secret."

An uncomfortable silence settled between them, one Charlie chose to interrupt with an uncomfortable question.

"So your mother was a drunk?"

"Yeah. My mom liked the bottle," she said, staring into her coffee cup to avoid the eye contact, thankful they'd managed to stray from talk of his wife. "I think I inherited that from her. I try to keep it under control. Aaron helped me with that."

"He doesn't like your drinking?"

"Not really that. He's not a substitute father figure or anything. He just lives clean. Goes to the gym. Is obsessed with food. I think he views food the same way I view hair."

"How's that?" Charlie asked.

"It's a way to be in control of things."

"Like writing."

"I suppose."

Over endless cups of coffee Charlie learned Ronnie had spent her life pushing limits . . . she drank early, did drugs early, had sex early. As a teenager she followed a band around the U.S. for a summer, was strip searched by U.S. border guards, got in a fist fight over a boy in Boston, watched a friend get stabbed in the shoulder with a penknife in New York, only to end up on a pay phone in Vermont, asking her very worried mother for some money so she could get on a bus and go home.

"Ronnie. Your life. I feel so . . ."

"Famous?"

"Stop it. I was going to say inadequate."

Ronnie smiled. "I was happy and loved and don't regret my youth at all. I had the ability to be reckless and careless and enjoy life."

"Unlike me. Afraid of everything."

"People like you better when you're afraid," she said mournfully. "More coffee?"

Charlie nodded despite the fact that he knew the caffeine was making him anxious. He watched as she got up from the table and walked toward the counter to request a couple more refills.

When she sat down again he stared at her intensely. "I think I may be falling in love with you, you know."

"How do you know?" she asked.

"It's just a feeling I have. I think you may bring out a masterpiece in me."

"That's what love is?" Ronnie laughed at this, but noticed immediately that Charlie appeared to be serious.

"I mean it. I could write an entire book about you. For you."

"No one's ever written anything for me but a prescription."

"Oh, that can't be true. I'm sure there are boys who you've been in love with who've got some Veronica poetry hidden in a desk drawer somewhere."

"Actually, I don't think I've ever really been in love. I mean, I've probably loved a hundred times, you know? But the kind of love that was the moment, the drama of it."

"Sometimes I think you should be the writer," Charlie said.

She laughed. "No. Far too much commitment."

"So commitment's not your thing either?"

"I was never really good at relationships. I tended to mistrust anyone who fell for me. Their love made them boring."

"What about Aaron?"

"Well, eventually I got things together. I went to hairdressing school and then I met Aaron at a bar when I was out with my girlfriends one night. Ladies night."

"One of those, eh?"

"No. Well. Yes," she laughed, blushing slightly.

"Nothing wrong with that."

"Well, there used to be nothing wrong with that."

"Did you know, right away, when you met him?" Charlie asked.

"Know what?" Ronnie asked genuinely.

"That you two were meant—"

"To be? Oh god no. I've never been romantic about that sort of stuff."

"Yes. I know. Hard-hearted. You hate feelings."

"I just find them messy. They're not really worth it."

"I have to disagree," Charlie said, smiling. "I bet under the right circumstances you could fall head over heels."

"How would you know? You've been in love with the same person most of your life."

Charlie ignored this. "I have to wonder how someone so reckless could be so guarded."

"Armour for fighting, I guess." Ronnie looked at him mournfully, apologetically.

It was Ronnie's recklessness that was most appealing to Charlie. He was in awe of her ability to put herself in compromising situations and come out unscathed. Her example suggested he might finally overcome the nagging fears and irrational thoughts that had plagued him his entire life. She seemed incapable of fear, a feeling he hoped would rub off on him when he touched the small of her back. Perhaps he was deluding himself, justifying her presence, but she had a calming disposition, this way of speaking to him when he was in the throes of irrationality, that successfully pulled him back.

"Did you know with Tamara? That you were meant for each other?" Ronnie asked suddenly.

"I like to think so. Yes. She made me feel safe."

"And how does she make you feel now?"

"I guess I don't feel safe anymore."

"And with me? How do you feel right now?" Ronnie asked.

Charlie smiled, reaching his hand across the table to touch her cheek. For the first time she didn't flinch or look around before his skin touched hers. "Scared. And safe."

75

(CHAPTER EIGHTEEN)

"You know how much I hate these things," said Ronnie, smoothing her hair flat in the bathroom mirror. She frowned at her appearance: she looked overtired.

"Yeah, but they're our friends. And if we were having a baby, you'd expect them to come, wouldn't you?" Aaron was already dressed and ready, leaning against the doorframe and impatiently watching Ronnie fuss with her appearance for what he hoped was a final time.

"No, Aaron, they're your friends," she said, now applying mascara with slow, methodical precision.

"Since when?"

"Since all our friends are your friends."

Aaron had little interest in arguing. He knew better than to engage in a fight with Ronnie when she was being irrational, and attributed her irritation to a lack of sleep or possibly a hangover from the half bottle of Merlot she had consumed with their steak dinner last night.

"Listen, we need to be there in ten minutes. You could have stated your objections to attending the shower when we got our invitation over a month ago."

"Maybe I didn't have objections a month ago. Maybe my objections stem from cervical biopsies and negative pregnancy tests. Ever consider that?"

"Oh Jesus, Ronnie. Why do you always have to be so fucking difficult?"

"Difficult? Me being sick and barren is not being difficult. It's being sick and barren."

"Now you're being overdramatic. You can't use this as a crutch all the time, you know. It won't get you anywhere."

"Fine. Let's just fucking go." Ronnie pushed past Aaron and into the front hall, where she grabbed her purse and jacket and angrily swung open the front door.

Aaron picked up the large, brightly wrapped gift from the kitchen table; a finely carved and painted wooden mobile, made up of stars and planets, that he had picked out and purchased himself.

The baby shower in Roncevalles was typical in every respect; the décor frosty cupcake colours and the attendees bright and cheery, clutching their champagne flutes of mimosa and snacking on crustless finger sandwiches. The mother-to-be lumbered around the packed living room with the glow of pride, even victory, as well-wishers threw their arms around her and told her how beautiful she looked at every opportunity.

Ronnie carefully avoided any conversations that involved motherhood, whether potential or current, but every instance of small talk tended to lean toward babies. She felt the creep of nausea overtake her and skulked off to the bathroom, where she found an array of children's bathtub toys prematurely installed in neat containers lining the tub. Ronnie sat warily on the closed toilet lid, wondering how people could be so committed to their choices, so sure of their monumental life changes as to celebrate them with lavish gatherings and too early purchases of tub toys.

She returned to the living room to seek out Aaron, who was laughing and punching the arm of the future father in a masculine gesture of congratulations that made her wince. The genuine pleasure and awe on his face momentarily crippled her, and she steadied herself on the back of the couch before draining an entire glass of champagne from a passing tray.

"Veronica?" a shrill voice called from behind her. She turned to see a woman she only vaguely recognized, her soft yellow hair pulled back into a buoyant ponytail that seemed to swing back and forth of its own volition. "Oh my god, Veronica! It's so wonderful to see you." The woman then leaned in for a hug that Ronnie accepted meekly. "I haven't seen you since high school," the blonde offered as a much-needed clue. "How are you doing?"

Ronnie searched her mind to place the woman's face, but only got as far as high school, incapable of finding a name or any other distinguishing characteristic. She continued the charade regardless, too exhausted by the entire scenario to do otherwise.

"Great. Really great."

"What are you doing now?"

"I'm a hairdresser."

"God, that's so interesting. You always were so different."

"So. How are you?"

"Oh wonderful. Me and Richard—you remember Richard, right?—we just bought a house in the east end. We were going to get a condo, but then I got pregnant with our second," she paused to make a gleeful gesture to her midsection, "and we just thought, why the hell not, right? Kids need a backyard, that's what they always say."

"Yup, that's what they say," Ronnie replied absently, desperately scanning the room for a fresh tray of champagne.

"And then Richard got promoted, and we were doing really well, so we decided just to go for it. And I don't even have to work anymore, which is fantastic, because all I really ever wanted to be was a mom anyway."

"That's great for you."

"So what about you? Married? Kids?"

"No. Neither."

"Well, certainly you at least have a boyfriend."

At least.

"We are getting older, Veronica. We can't go bar hopping our entire lives, now can we?" The woman erupted into laughter, patting Ronnie on the arm as if she was sharing in the joke.

With this Ronnie felt the nausea return, and what could have been the onset of hives.

"Listen, you'll have to excuse me. I've got an appointment this afternoon so me and my, um, Aaron, can't stay for long."

The blonde with her swinging ponytail seemed unfazed. "Well it was delightful to see you again, Ronnie. So nice to see you turned out okay."

What the fuck did that mean?

Ronnie unceremoniously beelined for Aaron, who was now locked in conversation with a group of men on the front porch. One of them was smoking a cigar and talking disdainfully about his overbearing wife. "You know, if it's not one thing with her, it's another. You know what I mean?"

Ronnie reached for Aaron's arm, interrupting the boisterous talk. "We have to leave," she managed to say.

"But we just got here."

"Please. Aaron. I can't breathe."

The other men on the porch averted their eyes.

Without saying anything, Aaron took Ronnie by the arm, down the porch steps, away from the blonde whose name she couldn't remember.

79

(CHAPTER NINETEEN)

At the end of the first week of February, Ronnie came to Charlie's office in the middle of the afternoon wearing a dress. A lemon-yellow dress, a strapless gauzy thing clearly meant for summer, a dress worn under her navy blue peacoat with knee-high black leather boots. When she came in, she locked the door behind her, then leaned back on it and breathed a heavy sigh. After a lengthy pause, wordlessly she walked to him, then sat down on his desk, facing him, her knees slightly parted, one on each side of him.

She let her coat slip from her shoulders slowly.

She said nothing, simply stared at him, his confused expression, her body slowly shifting weight from one pale, bare thigh to another.

"Ronnie—"

She put her fingertips on his mouth, gesturing for him to be silent. Charlie obliged and closed his eyes for a moment.

Charlie had never fully considered the reality of infidelity before Ronnie. He had of course fantasized about it, in the same way most people fantasize about dramatically quitting their jobs, selling their belongings, and wandering the world. Like anyone would, he had considered tearing off the clothes off a dozen or so beautiful undergrads, his mind wandering to places where they begged for a good grade, took him in their pink, glossy mouths, moaned while he thrusted, but it was never truly infidelity. Fantasizing about the nubile, tight flesh of vaguely intelligent, narcissistic undergrads was natural, and a world away from Ronnie on his desk in the middle of the afternoon.

Ronnie wasn't a girl in the third row of a classroom. Yes, she was pretty and earnest and at times naive, but a woman nonetheless. She had agency the girls in his fantasies didn't have.

Ronnie swung her legs onto the desk, closed her eyes, and lay down amongst his papers and books. Her right leg was bent and her left extended, her dark hair pushed back from her face, her mouth slightly open. Charlie, speechless, still seated at his desk, put his hand lightly, tentatively, on her knee, running his fingertips slowly along the inside of her thigh just as he had that night at the party.

The skin, the feel of it, was just as he remembered. Just as he had written.

He kissed the outside of her right knee first, his mouth lingering there while he took in the scent of drugstore body lotion and bar soap. Her skin was cold, and he was overcome by an urge to gently bite the flesh. He slid his hand up her thigh, pushing the hem of her dress up to her waist with it.

She arched her back and let out an encouraging sigh.

(CHAPTER TWENTY)

"You look different."

"Different?" Ronnie shifted uncomfortably on the couch while Aaron studied her expression with interest. She had been careful to shower and change when she had come home from Charlie's office, long before Aaron returned from errands and the gym. She had scrubbed every inch of her body carefully, buried her lemon-yellow dress in the bottom of the hamper, practiced her expression in the bathroom mirror to conceal any evidence that she had changed. Despite this she still felt the afternoon coated every inch of her, that if Aaron leaned in too close he would be able to smell the presence of someone else on her skin.

"Yeah. Different. Sunnier. I guess."

Ronnie laughed nervously. "Really?" The idea that she ever looked sunny was comical.

"Yeah." He paused thoughtfully. "It's really nice to see you happy. I've been worried about you lately. You've seemed distant."

"Yeah. You mentioned."

"And after the baby shower, I realized I haven't been all that fair to you." Aaron took a swig of his beer and casually looked back toward the television. He was being uncharacteristically attentive, and it immediately put Ronnie on edge.

"I guess I have been. Distant. Things have been hard."

"I'm sure you've been preoccupied with the baby. The tests. Glad to see you've come around to realizing that everything is going to be fine. That a lot of this stuff is in your head." He said this as if he were trying to convince himself that it were true.

When she was with Charlie she didn't think about babies or doctor's phone calls or cancer or failings. It was not true that she thought everything was going to be fine.

"Everything is going to be okay, Ronnie. We're going to be okay," he said sympathetically, reaching for her hand and stroking it lightly in the flicker of the television.

"I'd rather not talk about it if that's okay. I'm not trying to be difficult. I just think sometimes it's better to not talk about it."

"Okay." Aaron looked disappointed, but then perked up with a new idea. "Would you instead like to—" He looked at her suggestively, removing his hand from hers and running it up the side of her leg from his position on the couch. "You know. Take your mind off things?"

"Actually, Aaron. I'm really tired. I had a long day."

He looked wounded momentarily. "Yeah, really, what did you do?"

Ronnie was startled by the question, but managed to respond without flinching. "There were just some things I'd been putting off that I was meaning to take care of. They're done now."

Aaron didn't pursue this. He leaned in to kiss her softly, stroking her hair back from her face.

When Ronnie kissed Charlie she wanted to climb inside his mouth and sleep on his tongue. When Ronnie kissed Aaron she kept her eyes open.

Aaron returned his hand to his lap and his gaze to the television as a silence fell between them that would linger until both of them fell asleep on the couch.

(CHAPTER TWENTY-ONE)

The first time Charlie ever saw Tamara she was in a heated discussion with some fellow students at the back of a university bar. He was onstage, reading a poem with some difficulty, stumbling over a few lines, the crowd disinterested and barely noticing. Despite his nerves and hatred for public readings, he began to read in order to get her attention, as if the effort was only for her.

In large part the effort was unnecessary.

He had just retreated from the stage and back to his table of supportive if competitive friends, when she approached him.

"I really like that last poem you read," was Tamara's opening line.

"Oh yes?" Charlie smiled at her and handed her a glass, filling it with beer from his table's pitcher. His male companions looked at him knowingly, grinning their approval at the petite blonde who'd made her way over to compliment him.

"I didn't think you were all that interested. Whatever conversation you were having back there seemed pretty important," he said.

"What, you think a girl can't do multiple things at once?" She smiled widely, running her fingers through her wavy blonde hair in what could only be a flirtatious gesture.

"Why don't you have a seat," he said, motioning for a fellow writer to get up from his chair. He kindly obliged, and she sat snug against Charlie, taking a long gulp from her newly acquired glass. "So you like poetry, then?"

"Some of it."

"Do you study it?"

"No. I'm an economics major."

"Then what the hell are you doing here?"

"Drinking with you, apparently."

She raised her glass. He liked her confidence, the way she could easily walk away but chose not to.

"Well I'm glad you liked it."

"I did. Some poetry can be so pretentious."

"I think it depends on the person who's writing it."

"You seem nice enough," she said, offering another smile and then her name. "I'm Tamara."

"Charles Stern," he said, reaching out his hand.

She shook it slowly. "Maybe one day you'll write a poem about me as one of your many conquests, Mr. Stern."

"Oh, so you've heard about me."

"Everyone's heard about you. You're the anointed one, aren't you? The prodigy, I'm told."

Charlie hated that his reputation preceded him in so many circles, but Tamara seemed unfazed. "I imagine I'll write a whole book about you."

"And then I can be your only conquest."

"Well then I suppose you'll have to be my wife, no?"

Charlie's anxiety was pervasive. It was not the kind that people speak of when they say, "Oh, he has an anxious disposition." It was the kind that got people hospitalized. It was the kind that caused him to purchase endless hours of therapy and fistfuls of Ativan. It was the kind that made his jaw clench and his fists shake.

His anxiety was common knowledge in literary circles. Part of the charming writer identity he'd so successfully cultivated over the years. His publisher planned for his attacks on tours, booked hotels in close proximity to hospitals, and arranged exit strategies. Charlie was a problem on planes, at parties, in grocery stores. Meals at restaurants were delicate endeavours. And despite Charlie's constant yearning for escape from his life, remote locations were completely out of the question. The architecture of Charlie's mind could not be trusted to be stable.

Charlie failed at enduring the small details of life that most people found simple. Milk runs and subway rides. Ordering takeout and trips to the post office. Charlie was adept at locking himself in discreet bathroom stalls, vomiting and panting out his fears while curled up tightly on linoleum floors. His therapist assured him it was a product of his genius. Of his creative disposition. But Charlie felt that it was only his weakness that kept him out of the regular details of life. Anxiety in men was always a sign of a weakness they were incapable of mending with manly activities. The flesh around his middle suggested that athletics were not his chosen activity, and his reasonably happy and supportive wife was a sign of her resignation to his helplessness.

The anxiety arrived with the publication of his first collection of poems when he was merely twenty, no small feat for a boy barely a man, still in university, who charmed a small press publisher with his erotic musings on the girls he managed to meet in various literature classes and bed in various dorm rooms. Three days before it was to be printed Charlie threw up on a subway car, paralyzed by a convincing fear that he was at death's door.

The vomiting and dizzy spells came first. Then the sweaty, hyperventilating fits. Numbness in the extremities, increased heartbeat, depersonalization, a fear of losing complete control. Charlie became obsessed with exit strategies and hospital proximity. The subway, enclosed and deep underground without any reliable escape, became completely out of the question. The poisonous thoughts, irrational and pervasive, then ate at his brain and circled relentlessly, conjuring the wildest possibilities of his imminent demise—walls collapsing, dogs attacking, his insides riddled with disease. The characters in his book were sexy, reckless, fearless creatures, intent on the most enjoyable road to complete self-destruction. Charlie on the other hand became obsessed with intense self-preservation, every minor decision a possible doorway to complete disaster.

The only escape from the vice grip of doom was his ability to self-medicate, alcohol and marijuana having the uncanny ability

to provide him with an intoxicated window of reprieve where, although still sure his degradation and demise were imminent, he did not give a shit.

Labouring under the misapprehension that he was indeed dying while still only a teenager, he went to the walk-in clinic at the university only to find he was "troubled" and should be carted off the school counsellor.

A few years after he was diagnosed with generalized anxiety disorder, he met Tamara, who adapted to taking care of him quickly, in a way that suggested she actually took pleasure from it. She seemed to be looking for a wounded bird to care for, and Charlie launched into his twenties clinging to a diagnosed mental illness that excused his fragile nature.

"You were just made too sensitive for this world," she said when he confessed his panic attacks and obsessive thoughts to her one night over champagne post-sex. "That's what makes you beautiful."

The collection of poetry about all the girls that came before Tamara won acclaim and some small awards, and then a two-book deal, back when you could garner a two-book deal from a poetry collection. His success meant that Tamara began to cultivate a sense of pride that she knew all of the beloved poet's failings.

Tamara had been stunning then. She was petite and blonde and more intelligent than any woman he had ever met. She had a quickness about her, as if she was impossible to pin down, and impossible to intimidate. Her body was firm and curved and Charlie would run his fingers gingerly from knee to ribcage to drink her in. She laughed endlessly with her big beautiful laugh, managing to charm all of the same people Charlie managed to repel. She also had a stability about her, a firmness that echoed her solid, unyielding body, and Charlie clung closely to her in those early years of his illness. She acted as an anchor, and he would grasp her arm at events and readings, navigating those first flashes of success under her careful guidance.

While most assumed it was Tamara who benefited from Charlie's suddenly found fame, his private shame was that she was the only reason for it. She was the one who was able to push him through the tight spaces of life, to find him all the exits, to convince him that it wasn't cancer, that no one hated him, that the reviews were good even when they weren't. And when he couldn't be convinced, she coddled him, told him that it didn't matter, that there was much more to be done.

The ongoing, crippling anxiety was finally assuaged with a rather costly investment in intense cognitive behavioural therapy, a fee that Tamara's blue blood, WASPy parents had quietly paid when Tamara convinced them that this was the man she planned to marry, whether they liked it or not. They viewed it as an investment. It was important that he was well. Charlie would have bobbed along on an endless sea of despair—despair of his own making—if he hadn't met Tamara so early in life.

So naturally, he married her.

After he had been pulled from the worst, no one ever acknowledged the investment her parents made in the partial cure, and their marriage was blessed, however unenthusiastically. They married at city hall on a Friday afternoon in October. The bride wore grey and the groom threw up beforehand.

Charlie was loath to admit to himself that he married Tamara out of that sense of obligation and repayment.

It was because of Tamara that Charlie tattooed a small anchor of the inside of his wrist, right after they were married, a reminder that she was rooting him to earth. The tiny totem mocked him now with its early romanticism, its inability to predict a mundane future.

Noah was conceived more than a decade after they first met. They had had no intention of having a child, initially because both were focused on their careers and then later because their relationship had soured. He was an accident, but an accident that was never acknowledged because marriage made calling a child a mistake impossible. There was money, stability, and no reason not to have Noah beyond crippling fear, so they went ahead.

When he was born, Noah had the immediate ability to bring Tamara and Charlie closer together. Ten fingers, ten toes—this squirming pink mass that proved they could make something together that actually *worked*. He was a perfect, beautiful child, and Tamara was suddenly beautiful again, her bitterness subsiding. Charlie stayed home with Noah when Tamara went back to work after a brief mat leave. The newborn gave Charlie purpose, made him feel like he was finally contributing to a marriage that had risked falling apart via pure malaise. His anxiety dissipated because he had something real to worry about, something that depended on him to be fearless.

And Charlie was excited to discover that while he was generally terrible at being alive, he was actually very good at being a father.

But as Noah grew older and missed the developmental milestones, Charlie's anxiety returned. It came at first like a slight tap on the shoulder, tiny waves of doubt that slipped in, and Charlie knew the paralysis would come again. It was only a matter of time. He watched his child, the one that had been a symbol of so much false hope for both of them, and knew only doom would come.

Noah was late to walk and speak, refused to smile, and didn't have interest in other children. He would scream and cry without reason, organize his toys methodically, and although he could count beyond a hundred at only twenty months, he couldn't create sentences or respond to his name. When Noah was finally diagnosed with autism, Charlie learned the statistic that eighty percent of parents of autistic children divorce, and he took that as a challenge.

In crowded spaces and dark theatres, Tamara had become adept at pulling Charlie out of the tight corners of life, but it was Tamara who wept uncontrollably for days when they learned Noah's fate. Charlie held her, and though he felt guilty for thinking it, he was happy that for once she was the wounded bird and he would be forced to take care of both of them.

(CHAPTER TWENTY-TWO)

After the day Veronica went to Charlie's office and laid on his desk as an invitation, she began to think about kissing Charlie with unending frequency. It was the kind of kissing that leads nowhere and everywhere. The groping, desperate kisses of teenagers before they've explored anything else to do with their bodies. People who have fallen into the motions of predictable sex . . . the kind you roll into while drunk or exhausted . . . they yearn only for the aimless grinding of youth.

The thoughts would leave her panting and nauseated.

Ronnie closed her eyes in the bathtub, behind a locked door, while Aaron was in the house, and thought of Charlie in a variety of inappropriate ways and a variety of inappropriate situations. Her capacity to fantasize amazed her, and the frantic detail in which she did disturbed her. After years of living with Aaron—after the unending, mechanical efforts to breed—fantasy had left her, and she welcomed it back with sticky, sweaty fervour.

Now that they had slept together, their coffee dates seemed foolishly innocent, so they graduated to later evenings, to cocktails, with more elaborate lies and more obscure locations. They had something to hide now, so they needed a way of numbing that feeling and a place to hide it that wasn't a campus coffee shop.

Ronnie would watch foolishly transfixed, a voyeur, as he lifted his pint glass to his lips. She would reimagine that single action over and over, recreating it in complex detail and at varying speeds. She would review the action as if they were both in slow motion, frozen in a slow, creeping, clandestine moment, over and over again. She wanted to sink her teeth into the fleshy pink of his bottom lip. She found herself putting her fingers in her mouth while he spoke, gnawing at them, pinching them between her teeth, occupying her tongue, trying to stave off the urge to reach across the table and swallow him whole.

"When I'm with you, Charlie, I just want to kiss you over and over and over again."

He never talked about anything particularly interesting, or at least anything she could fully understand, but it failed to matter. Ronnie knew nothing about poetry nor was she particularly interested in it, and she could tune out the stories of university things and university people she cared little about. While his lips moved she took the time to scrutinize every reason she wanted to taste them. Certainly she'd considered that her attraction to Charlie was absurd, but beyond that the visceral, nauseous nature of the desire was foreign to her. Charlie had an ability to make her sick to her stomach, her head light, her clichéd knees weak. She wasn't sure how she'd managed. She'd spent so many nights lying next to Aaron wondering if this was the way things went. She'd spent so many mornings in bed with her thoughts, imagining things she could never do with Aaron, the kinds of things that Aaron would never believe her capable of. Things she could do with Charlie.

It seemed that Aaron's body was always turned away from her, curled up facing the wall, breathing deep. He fell asleep so many hours before her, and as a result woke up so many hours before she did. He chastised her for this, lightly called her lazy in a way she loathed. It was the kind of criticism Aaron would raise jokingly in front of mutual friends, thinking he was being loving and comical, but Ronnie would seethe with anger as their brunch or dinner party companions laughed jovially over her laziness. As she became more and more enamoured with Charlie and his every gesture, she began to despise Aaron. His voice became grating and his requests intolerable.

In her mind she had already left Aaron. In her mind she had moved out completely . . . packed up every last thing and found a new space in the crook of Charlie's neck. In her mind every piece of her was Charlie's, broken or otherwise. And was it enough that she was his in her mind? Would she have to sever herself in real life as well? Because the idea of dividing up her life and telling those laughing, joking brunch companions destroyed her even when she simply thought about it. The heartbreak of severing she could tolerate. It was the logistics of moving on, the shame of judgment she couldn't bear.

She pondered these things while she watched his mouth, wet with ale, that pink shiny mouth, that beautiful plump—

"Ronnie, are you even listening to me?"

"Yes Charlie. The university. They're screwing you."

"Nice synopsis."

"I'm sorry. I'm distracted."

"Where are you?"

"I'm sorry. I was thinking about Aaron."

The words, the lie, came out of her mouth before she had a chance to consider them. Charlie frowned. Ronnie wasn't entirely sure why she had said it. Perhaps to wound him? To remind them both about their bad behaviour? She often said Aaron's name out loud to remind herself that he wouldn't want her to be there. When she was with Charlie, it was easy to forget that Aaron existed, that he kissed her goodnight and kissed her good morning every day. The acknowledgement of his existence was important.

"Why do you always have to bring him up?"

"I don't *always* bring him up."

"That was the third time today."

"I bring him up because he's at home waiting for me. Because he thinks I'm 'running errands.'"

"He's not waiting for you, Ronnie. He doesn't know you exist."

"Fuck you."

"No, fuck you."

Charlie was being cruel and Ronnie knew it. He'd managed to build a caricature of this man he'd never met, someone who he believed to be a despicable, abusive, neglectful man, in order to justify the cuckolding. Every so often he'd casually suggest that Aaron didn't really love her, or that if he did, he wasn't very good at it. Despite Ronnie's assertions that Aaron was a "good person," Charlie continually convinced himself that Aaron was an abusive monster. She knew it was because it made their actions easier for him to bear, that he never considered himself to be the type of man who would sleep with someone else's . . .

"If I could have you I wouldn't neglect you."

But you can have me, Charlie. You just don't want me.

Charlie tipped back his pint dramatically, empowered by his own statement, and motioned impolitely for the waitress to bring him another.

"Don't do that."

"Do what?"

"Motion at the waitress like she's a fucking servant. It's like you think anyone who doesn't have some creative calling is beneath you."

"Creative calling? What are you even talking about?"

"I'm not beneath you, you know."

"Oh, is that what this is about?"

"Don't say it like that. Like you've known it all along."

"I don't think you are beneath me, Ronnie."

"And he doesn't neglect me."

"Why are you even defending him? Half the time you come and meet me you've been crying or you start crying. If you're so miserable all the time, I don't understand why you don't leave."

"Probably for the same reasons you don't leave."

Charlie broke eye contact and began to fidget.

"I want to go," Ronnie said.

"I just ordered another beer."

"Then stay and drink your beer. I want to go."

CHAPTER TWENTY-THREE

"What's wrong with the dryer?" Charlie asked, coming up the stairs from the basement clutching a pile of his wet clothes.

"Maybe if you were around more, you would know that the dryer needs fixing, Charlie," Tamara replied from the kitchen, her voice thick with resentment.

Charlie pretended not to hear, dumping his damp shirts, pants, and underwear on the living room rug and collapsing on the couch. He stared past the television, which was showing the six o'clock news piece on the dangers of escalators, through the glass sliding door and into the backyard.

"Please tell me you're not just going to leave that pile of wet clothing there on the rug, Charles," Tamara said.

"No. I'm not going to just leave it there. I'm going to leave it there for now."

"I'm happy to get someone in to fix the dryer during the day, Mrs. Stern," Amanda offered, stirring a pot of soup on the stove for Noah's dinner. She seemed consistently unmoved by their bickering, perhaps because it was happening more frequently, and with much more mutual disdain. Amanda had a knack for making herself a casual, unobtrusive observer of their marital woes, and Charlie often wondered what kind of conversations she had with friends over beers about the disastrous marriage she had a hand in maintaining. How she promised them and herself she'd never turn out that way.

"Absolutely not. It is most certainly not your job to get the dryer fixed. Charlie, you need to get it together. I can't do everything."

"That's right. Because I do nothing."

It seemed to Charlie that Tamara was angry all the time,

frustrated that he was never around, never contributing, never aware of the larger concerns of the family. It seemed to Charlie that Tamara had been this way not just since he had met Veronica, but for years and years, perhaps since the very beginning.

"I'll take care of it, Amanda," Charlie said flatly without turning his head toward the kitchen where she and Tamara were preparing dinner.

"Unlikely," Tamara added.

She had punished him for so long that he couldn't remember where and when it started. For so long he had been a disappointment that he didn't know how to be anything else.

The nightly news was now reporting on a shooting that had happened at a high school in the east end. Charlie thought for a moment about how pointless damp clothes on the living room rug were in the face of a crazed gunman.

"You know, Charlie, Amanda has been forced to take Noah's things to the laundromat. That's really not fair to her."

"I heard you the first time, Tamara. I'll get it done."

"It's okay, Mrs. Stern."

"No, it's really not."

"If you could do something about that sooner rather than later—you know if you're not too busy with that book you're writing every fucking night."

With each strained conversation, more of his marriage was chipped away into a rubble they both wilfully ignored. Where once Tamara lived to care for his neurosis, to celebrate his gift, to proclaim herself the wife of a writer, she had become wary of his neediness. Where once he felt important to another human being, he now felt like a burden unworthy of being carried.

Perhaps it had always been this way and only in having Ronnie had he noticed.

"Really, Mrs. Stern. It's no trouble. I'll get someone in to repair the dryer first thing."

Charlie breathed a heavy sigh and wished Amanda had not pushed. That she would shut up. He watched in the reflection of the glass door as Tamara furiously and wordlessly retreated upstairs, slamming the bedroom door.

"I'm sorry, Mr. Stern."

Charlie switched off the television. "You can go home now, Amanda. I'll feed Noah. If you could pour me a glass of Scotch before you go I'd be grateful."

(CHAPTER TWENTY-FOUR)

RONNIE

In those naked moments in his office, while Charlie was drawing lines with his fingertips across my skin, I would tell him stories about my childhood. He encouraged it, asked me questions like "when did you first think you were in love?" and "tell me about your first kiss." While he would run his hand lightly over my breast, my belly, my shoulder, he would watch me speak like he was an eager student in a classroom.

High school stories seemed to be his favourite. He loved hearing about me in a Catholic school uniform, in a wool beret and fingerless gloves, smoking weed with the boys.

"Weren't you ever worried? Weren't you ever afraid?" he would ask.

He would kiss the parts of me that he had touched and tell me that if he had known me then, he would have fallen deeply in love with me. And I knew he was already deeply in love with me.

I began to know the right stories to tell. He was aroused by my recklessness, would sigh heavily when I told him stories of me drunkenly scaling fences or stripping my clothes off in the rain. I would pick out moments of my life where I pushed hard at people who loved me and the people who did not. He had a fetish for me breaking things in the name of feeling alive, I assumed because he lived in a fear of his own creation every day.

"You're an amazing woman, Veronica," he would say, finally kissing me on the mouth, long and deep, pressing himself against me, his thigh slipping between mine.

Inevitably after a story was told, we would make love in a way that was soft and sweet, in contrast to the usual desperate groping of our initial interactions.

It was the violence in me that Charlie desired the most.

(CHAPTER TWENTY-FIVE)

"Happy Valentine's Day, beautiful." Aaron held up a small box, wrapped in heart-printed paper and tied with an obnoxiously large, shiny red bow.

"I thought we agreed we weren't going to give each other anything? With saving for the baby and all that."

Despite their recent lack of sex and her general lack of fertility,

Ronnie had made an appointment with her doctor and gone back on the pill earlier that week. They expressed vague concern over her precarious health but she insisted.

"Weren't you and Aaron planning—" her doctor asked.

"Things change," she said and her doctor, of course, didn't persist.

The last thing she wanted was to get pregnant and then have to figure out whether it was Aaron's or Charlie's.

She kept the pills in a cigar box at the bottom of a ten-gallon plastic Rubbermaid container full of moth-eaten clothes in her closet so Aaron would never find them. She refused to admit to herself that Charlie was the reason for that. All she knew was the moment she had drunk that shot of peach schnapps, any interest in reproducing had left her completely.

"Yeah, but this is kind of for the baby," he said, beaming.

The baby. The baby. The baby. Sometimes Charlie called her baby. After she came on his desk he had stroked her forehead, called her "good girl" over and over while she panted and squirmed.

Ronnie ripped at the paper to find, much to her horror, a black velvet ring box. Aaron suddenly descended from his seat at their tiny kitchen table to one knee on the linoleum floor. She resisted a sudden urge to vomit, swallowing hard, and clicked the box open to reveal a small diamond ring.

To cope, she made a joke. "I don't think a baby will be able to wear this, Aaron."

"No, silly. I mean that the baby gets married parents. A baby needs married parents, don't you think? And stop making jokes."

"No, actually, I don't think that a baby needs married parents." Ronnie was surprised it came out. Aaron's face sank.

"Aaron, I'm sorry, I didn't mean—I just thought we decided—"

Ronnie had always been convinced that a marriage, or any commitment, that was a reaction to illness, tragedy, threat, or strife was always suspect.

"Please don't speak, Ronnie. Let me do this." His tone was slightly harsh despite his smiling.

Her only thought was that Aaron was proposing because he knew Ronnie was having an affair. That was the only explanation. He had never been interested in marriage before, so he must have somehow discovered that she had gone to Charlie's office in the middle of the afternoon and removed her pink cotton underwear on his desk, that she had let Charlie touch her until she came, that Charlie had firmly clasped his hand over her mouth while she had done so to prevent any of the professors or students in nearby offices from hearing.

He must have proposed because he knew that she had loved it, that the guilt she had read about and been told about that came over people after they had cheated never came over her. That she had not regretted it and would likely do it again, and again, and again, if only because having a secret of that magnitude made her feel like she had an identity severed from the life she shared with him. A life that, if she was honest with herself, she could never get comfortable in.

Of course Aaron did not know what she was really doing with her afternoons and evenings, but he had felt her distance, the way she occasionally flinched when he touched her, ever so slightly, and had opted to solve it by giving her what he assumed every woman would want.

"You've just seemed off lately, with our not being able to have a baby and all. But, honey, I'm sure it'll happen for us. I promise it'll happen for us."

Aaron removed the ring from the box and took Ronnie by her

left hand. She resisted the urge to pull away. She stared at a space on his forehead simply because it was much too difficult to look him in the eye.

"Veronica Suzanne Kline, will you be my wife?"

She said yes because it was the quickest way to get him to stand up.

(CHAPTER TWENTY-SIX)

The next morning, Ronnie woke up to a pile of wedding magazines arranged carefully on the kitchen table. They were purchased from the convenience store on the corner and Aaron had left them there, a less-than-subtle hint to start planning that suggested Aaron recognized her disinterest.

Ronnie stood in the kitchen in her blue striped bathrobe, and stared at them for a full three minutes before she managed to put the kettle on the stove. The smiling models in their gleaming white dresses and gleaming white smiles mocked her, staring accusingly, and she managed to burn a slice of whole grain toast while transfixed by what was obviously a fourteen-year-old girl holding a bunch of red balloons while running through a field in a dress that resembled a overly iced cake.

The smiling. Ronnie couldn't take all the smiling.

The idea of having the nuptial pornography in the house was intolerable, so instead she brought them with her to the salon, disposing of them among the endless celebrity gossip rags and fashion tomes women read while they were waiting for their highlights to set.

Lisa immediately eyed the magazines suspiciously. "Hey, Rons, you got something to tell me?" She smiled slyly, fussing over her fuchsia-dyed hair in a mirror and raising a penciled-in eyebrow. Ronnie focused on sweeping a hair into a neat pile, busying herself to avoid Lisa's suspicious looks in the mirror.

"Oh that? God no. I just thought all the brides that come in here would appreciate some guidance. If I have to do an up-do with baby's breath one more time I'll puke. Giving them other options is an investment in my sanity."

"You're fucking lying."

"I'm not."

"Well, thank god for that. I thought you were joining the sheep."

Ronnie swallowed, leaning the broom against the wall. "No. Of course not. Just work research."

Lisa remained unconvinced. "Hey, you and Aaron ever think of getting married?" she asked, removing an eyebrow pencil from her purse and going to work on her left brow.

"Why would we bother? We practically are anyway."

"I didn't ask you that." Lisa had this uncanny ability to know exactly what was going on. When Ronnie had launched into her affair with Charlie it was Lisa who had noticed and commented that she had "a glow about her." "You getting laid more?" she had asked.

The thing Ronnie appreciated most about Lisa was that she was incapable of judgment. As someone who didn't believe in "too much information," and who often subjected her clients to stories about her various sexual experiments and implements, nothing had the ability to shock.

"Okay. Aaron asked me to marry him last night."

"And there you go. The truth comes out." Lisa didn't even look up from her makeup application.

"Sorry. I just haven't really processed it. I spent a chunk of my morning looking at pictures of preteen faux Stepford wives-to-be," Ronnie said, gesturing to the magazine pile.

"They're better off here. I've seen many a good woman get sucked in by that crap." Lisa decided she was done her primping and collapsed heavily into the chair behind her. She spun the chair in Ronnie's direction dramatically. "So he, like, asked you, asked you? Like down on one knee with a ring asked you?" Lisa was containing her natural inclination to jump up and scream over this news.

"Yes. He proposed. Like they do in the movies, I guess. All very traditional."

"God. Finally."

102

"Yes. Finally. I guess."

"Sorry. I take it from the fact you're not wearing said ring that you're not exactly pleased?"

Ronnie looked down at her naked ring finger and self-consciously made a fist. She had removed it and put it in the coin pouch of her wallet before she had left for work that morning.

"It's not that. I just—"

"It is just that. It's all over your face. Girl, you are not happy about this development."

Lisa's client, an elderly lady whose short lavender hair was set in foamy pink rollers under the hair dryer, was clearly enthralled with Ronnie's apparent distaste with her partner's proposal. She lifted the dryer ever so slightly so she could survey Ronnie's expression.

"It's not that I don't want to. I just don't see the point."

"The point is that you are in love. Unless of course you're not in love. Which is fine, but another conversation entirely."

"I'm in love. Of course I'm in love. We're in love. Whole lotta love."

"Convincing. So I suppose a congratulatory hug is out of the question?" Lisa raised her tattooed arms mockingly.

"No, really. I'm happy. Of course. I'm very happy with Aaron."

"Well, I better be a fucking bridesmaid or you're dead to me."

Lisa lunged forward and wrapped Ronnie in a large hug. Ronnie collapsed into her, holding on for just a bit too long.

"I've got you," Lisa said quietly and knowingly, holding her tight.

"You know, dear," the woman in the foam rollers offered, "a proposal is what every girl dreams of. You should count yourself among the lucky ones."

After her late morning shift was over Ronnie went straight to Charlie's office, locked the door behind her, and straddled him in his desk chair. She placed her palm over his mouth and stared at him for a few moments.

He pulled her palm from his mouth. "Ronnie. I missed you," he said.

"Shhh."

A few students came to the door and knocked while the two of them kissed clumsily, frantically, wordlessly. Ronnie never mentioned Aaron's proposal, never mentioned much of anything, and did not wear the engagement ring.

She thought of it momentarily while she removed her dress over her head and then unhooked her bra in the soft light of Charlie's office.

"Charlie, don't ever leave me, okay?" she said as her bra dropped to the floor.

"Never."

CHAPTER TWENTY-SEVEN

After the next batch of tests came back as abnormal Ronnie was asked to the hospital for further tests. As predicted, a biopsy. For cervical cancer. Ronnie said the words to herself over and over again until they sounded normal, comfortable, no problem at all.

Biopsy for cervical cancer. Biopsy for cervical cancer. Biopsy for cervical cancer.

"Isn't this common? Doesn't this happen all the time?" Aaron had asked. The familiar refrain. There was a tiny expression or fear, maybe panic, that flashed across his face while she reassured him that yes, it was routine. At least that what the doctor had said.

"Lisa tells me lots of women go through it," she said, despite the fact that she'd never met any women who had.

"Well, that's good that you're dealing with it then. Before we start a family. That everything is healthy."

Ronnie found it strange that Aaron had said "everything" instead of "you."

Aaron drove her to the appointment at the hospital on University Avenue and dutifully read the pamphlets in the waiting room. Ronnie could not help but notice the terrified expressions of the other women who sat stiffly around her, waiting for their names to be called.

Aaron held her hand until she was ushered into a tiny, fluorescent lit examination room and greeted by a male med student who looked no older than nineteen. He asked her detailed and at times insensitive questions, making sporadic notes on his clipboard and occasionally grunting incomprehensible responses to her answers.

"How many sexual partners have you had in the past year?"

She was afraid to answer the question honestly, but when she did the boy with the clipboard seemed unfazed.

"When was the last time you had sexual intercourse?"

It had taken her many weeks to even think about washing the lemon-yellow dress. She hadn't had the time, nor the strength, to take it to the laundromat, and when she finally did she couldn't bear to rinse it clean. When she finally sorted the laundry to take it down she removed the dress from the pile and hid it next to the birth control pills in her closet where it had remained ever since.

"All right, Miss Kline. I'm going to need you to remove your pants and underwear for me."

Her paper gown crinkled as she lay down on the table and waited for a doctor she'd never seen before to return with a new collection of med students, all of whom spoke in hushed tones with weak smiles and never made eye contact.

"Are you ready, Veronica?"

She nodded.

(CHAPTER TWENTY-EIGHT)

There was something truly intoxicating about their clandestine meetings, the way they drank together in financial district bars, surrounded by people they assumed were lawyers and bankers, a sea of suits to save them from being caught by colleagues and friends. They were invisible, safe among the blues and greys of the mundane power struggles and lecherous socializing. There was something irrelevant about the two of them in that environment, their awkwardness and lack of sleek costuming. They didn't belong and were therefore largely ignored.

That day, in that particular bar, running her foot lightly along the inside of Charlie's calf, gave Ronnie a secret thrill. The act, dangerous and partially visible to people who couldn't care less, reminded her of the way things used to be between her and Aaron before they became so predictable.

Ronnie reconsidered. "I think it's important we don't touch in public," she said suddenly, putting down her glass and folding her hands on the table in front of her. The statement was more of a question: she was unsure of the rules.

"We can do it accidentally?" Charlie asked, smiling.

"Of course," she said.

"We can do it covertly?"

"Of course." She returned the toe of her shoe to the inside of his calf.

"Well, that's a relief."

"I just don't want to be reckless."

"Yes. Discretion. Discretion is key," he laughed.

"It's not really funny, Charlie. I just don't want to be unkind."

Her pointed toe continued up to his knee, where he reached for it, slipped his hand into the cuff of her jeans, and held her tiny ankle in his hand. "Of course. We should always be respectful. Adult."

"Grown-ups."

They both nodded furiously, comically, despite the fact that neither of them had ever been capable of being grown-up or adult about anything else in their lives. Cheating was of course unacceptable, but their ability to hide it, their kindness in not shaming their partners with their actions, somehow made it justifiable. The covenant of their secret made them grown-up. Made them respectful, empathetic.

"I want you," Charlie said quietly when the server had cleared their glasses.

"Not today, Charlie."

"Ronnie, please," he gripped her calf under the table, pulling her toward him with such force that she had to brace herself against the table.

"Charlie, you know I can't today. Aaron's expecting me."

He pouted like a child.

"Soon." Ronnie bit her lip, feeling the burn of his fingertips on her skin.

"Tell me when."

"I'm not sure. It'll depend when I can get away."

"When you can get away from Aaron?"

Ronnie pulled her foot from Charlie's grasp and adjusted herself at the table. "Don't do that. You know what I mean."

"I want you to get away from Aaron forever."

"I don't know if I can do that yet," Ronnie replied solemnly.

Ronnie could admit that she despised Aaron for his tender way, the way he rubbed her back or held her hand. Charlie did not hurt her, but his need for her exceeded his need to be gentle. She was grateful for this. Aaron had always coddled her as though she was a child, and he worried and doted and took care of everything as if she were incapable of doing so.

Once she and Charlie had slept together on his desk in the middle of the afternoon, what she could not admit was that she would never leave Aaron. That she could not leave Aaron. That she had to marry Aaron. That despite all her love and desire for Charlie, real life dictated that all they would ever have was clandestine meetings and concealed touching beneath barroom tables. Two children could never be together. What Ronnie could not admit was that despite Charlie's combative pleading, she was probably okay with that.

"I should probably go," Ronnie said, looking at her watch and pulling out her purse to pay the bill.

Together Charlie and Ronnie left the Bay Street bar and rabidly kissed goodbye in an alley adjacent to a parking garage.

Hungry and elated, Charlie arrived at his quiet home in the Annex to find his wife in the living room, reading a novel. She was without makeup, her hair wet from a bath, wearing nothing but a light cotton robe.

"Where have you been?" she asked, not looking up from her book. "You missed dinner."

"Where's Noah?" he asked, ignoring her question. He stood above her, his face expressionless.

Tamara removed her glasses and placed them on the arm of the couch. "Out with Amanda for a few hours. I needed a break. He was acting out again. We really need to talk about the way he's been lately. If there's something we should do. If there's something we can do."

Charlie said nothing, just stared down at her blankly.

"Charlie? What's with you? Where have you been?"

Buoyed by afternoon drinks, Charlie kneeled before her and gently pulled the cord on her robe until it fell open, revealing her nakedness beneath. She sat motionless, exposed, a look of both concern and breathless anticipation on her face. She resisted the urge to pull the robe to her chest, confused by his intensity.

"Charlie . . ."

He put two fingers to her lips to silence her and then gently pulled the robe from her shoulders until it fell around her waist. Gripping a fistful of damp hair at the back of her head, he leaned in to kiss her.

She said nothing, did not fight him . . . simply fell back into the throw pillows and closed her eyes as he undid his belt.

CHAPTER TWENTY-NINE

The English department at the university seemed really to enjoy Aaron's catering. So much so that he was invited back to cater another event in March. Again he asked Ronnie to assist and again she obliged, pulling back on that snug-fitting black dress and toting giant platters of pre-prepared food from their aging brown station wagon and into yet another Annex home.

"Do you ever think it's funny that people from Parkdale feed people in the Annex?" she asked.

"No, Ronnie, I think it's a job," Aaron snapped.

"It was just a question."

Aaron caught himself, paused for a moment. "I'm sorry. You know how these things stress me out."

But she didn't know how these things stressed him out.

Aaron had been on edge for the month since the engagement began. He had never been one to talk about his feelings, so instead he became distant and testy. Ronnie actually benefited from his non-confrontational attitude. Her late nights and unexplained absences never became an issue. She was constantly "running errands," and Aaron never asked questions.

When they were inside Ronnie adjusted her dress and checked her teeth in the reflection of a butter knife while Aaron unpacked hors d'oeuvres in the sprawling stainless steel and granite kitchen, a kitchen they could never afford. Things were strained between them, so they found reprieve by acting like co-workers, neatly arranging plates of food with intense accuracy. Occasionally Aaron would correct Ronnie and she would not argue, simply following his direction without emotion. She hadn't the strength nor the interest to argue with him while he was working.

When Aaron was satisfied that everything was in order, he finally softened. "Thanks for helping me again."

"That's what I'm here for."

"No," he said, pulling her into an embrace. "I really do appreciate it."

As she uncomfortably remained in his arms for a moment she acknowledged it was inevitable that she would run into Charlie that evening, despite the fact that the two of them rarely discussed their schedules. She didn't want to know about Noah's therapy appointments or the dinner parties that he and Tamara attended with his literary friends, anyway. She especially didn't want to hear about the fact that Tamara and Charlie were still fucking. That they were fucking even more now that his libido was provoked by Ronnie in his life, sparked by the resentment that now filled their lives and marital bed. That he closed his eyes and thought of Ronnie while he came. It hurt too much to think about it. She would prefer to pretend that he only spent time with her.

The idea of running into him at the party made her ill. Not only because Aaron was there and there was a chance of the two of them meeting, but also because they had never, since that first meeting, been together around people who weren't strangers. The crowd tonight would care if they knew. Knew that they had been together, that she was the "other woman." Ronnie was sure she could successfully make it through the evening without incident, but not entirely sure that Charlie could do the same. In a world of Bay Street bars and casual walks, onlookers only saw them as people in love, or as nothing at all.

She was reassured of her appearance and relieved of her discomfort by Aaron, whose mood had lightened enough to notice her concerned expression and tell her she looked "perfect." He gave her a light kiss on the cheek and sent her out into the living room with a cheese plate. "Charm them and they'll have us back."

Ronnie was indeed charming with guests despite her discomfort. She glided around the room, smiling and chatting as if nothing was on her mind. She even managed to coyly flirt with the older gentlemen, who called her "sweetheart" and "delightful." All the while she could feel the disdainful gaze of Sarah, Charlie's meddling colleague, but managed to put it out of her mind.

When Charlie finally arrived, he did so with two waify girls, both of whom were approaching six feet tall and who couldn't have been more than twenty years old. They wore scarves and layers and talked nonsense about little-known books while reapplying cherry lip gloss, and Ronnie hated them both immediately. She hated the way they carried themselves unselfconsciously, that despite the fact that they were so out of place at the party they failed to care, tipping back countless drinks and gorging their impossibly thin bodies on cheese and thinly sliced meat. She noticed one of the girls had a sprawling butterfly tattoo on her left shoulder that was exposed each time her oversized boat-necked shirt fell down her arm. They laughed too loudly at Charlie's jokes and touched him on the shoulder at every opportunity. Ronnie was not unfamiliar with the fact that young women worshipped both Charlie and his prose, but seeing it on display was too much to bear. One of them had even taken to calling him "Chuck."

Ronnie peered at the group of them through a slight gap in the double kitchen doors, watched as Charlie placed his hand lightly on their waists while they chatted, watched them lean in close for secrets.

Up until that point it hadn't actually occurred to Ronnie that Charlie might have done this before. She had naively assumed she was his first extramarital infatuation, certainly his first clandestine affair, but watching him position himself comfortably between two women half his age and twice his height set off a flood of worry that she was merely a name on a very long list.

Tamara was jealous of girls like Ronnie. Ronnie was jealous of girls like these smooth-skinned, fertile hangers-on. Girls terrified of pregnancy.

She tapped her foot impatiently on the tiled floor.

"Can I bring something out for you?" Ronnie asked Aaron abruptly.

"No, sweetie. It's okay. I know you hate being here. Just have a seat and relax."

"No really. *I want to.* I want to help."

Aaron, too distracted and flustered by further preparation to notice her distress, gestured toward a platter piled with cookies. White chocolate raspberry macadamia nut and double mint chocolate chunk. "Those need to go out."

She picked up the gleaming silver platter and pushed dramatically through the double doors, beelining for Charlie and his entourage despite the numerous hands that groped at her platter.

"Cookie?"

Charlie turned to meet Ronnie's gaze. The anger visible in her face made the towering hipster twins cease their giggling.

"Ronnie. Hi. I—"

"I'm sorry, sir. Have we met? I'm quite certain we haven't. I'm the caterer's wife. Cookie?"

"You're not the caterer's wife."

"Yet," she spat.

Charlie took this as a threat, not understanding that her engagement ring sat in a soap dish in the host's kitchen, that she had excused its removal with hand washing rather than confessing to Aaron she was concealing the news from one of the party-goers.

"You should really have a cookie. The caterer is *infinitely* talented."

Ronnie was not usually one for jealousy, never once questioned the girls that Aaron occasionally name-dropped, but for some reason Charlie and his companions had provoked a rage in her that was blinding. An unfamiliar feeling that made her want to break something. Including the faces of his admirers.

The girls themselves were mostly oblivious to the drama that was unfolding in front of them. Both leaned in for a cookie, lifting them from opposite ends of the platter poised at neck height between Charlie and Ronnie. One blonde and the other brunette, they book-ended Charlie and shoved the cookies in their mouths, letting out satisfied sighs after they swallowed. Crumbs descended from their lips and into their revealing tops.

"Chuck, you should have a cookie, they're so fucking good," the breathy blonde gasped, gripping his arm and leaning into his shoulder. The brunette broke off a piece of hers and offered it to him, fully expecting him to eat it from her fingers.

"These would be awesome if you were high," the brunette added.

"Yes, *Chuck*. They really are *delicious*," Ronnie responded, her gaze unwavering, the platter perched on her fingers as if she might hurl it at any moment. She was aware now that some of the more perceptive dinner guests were staring, including the ever-present Sarah with her unwavering suspicions about Charlie and Ronnie's relationship.

"Ronnie. Please don't. Not here."

"Then shall we find a hotel room?"

The girls both turned toward him in near comical unison.

"Veronica. Stop it. Now."

"You should really meet the caterer. Shall I bring him out? So you can compliment the chef?"

Aaron was safely tucked away in the kitchen. He rarely made his way into the party during events, thinking it unprofessional.

"I'm sure that won't be necessary."

"You have no fucking idea how necessary it is."

"Stop it. We're just having fun here. Relax."

"Oh, really? We're just having fun?"

"Don't embarrass yourself, Ronnie."

Ronnie dropped the platter on the ground in front of them just as the brunette groped for another cookie "to save for later."

Ronnie stayed within earshot long enough to hear the blonde with the butterfly tattoo say, "What the fuck was her problem?"

Charlie got into his office the following morning with a blinding hangover. His twenty-something-year-old companions had encouraged him to keep up with them, and by three a.m. they were lying in the middle of a field on U of T campus drinking Fireball whisky straight from the bottle.

He recalled stealing a copy of his own poetry book from a bookshelf at the party and later doing a dramatic reading of it aloud to them while they clapped and giggled and said, "Oh Chuck, you're a fucking genius." He couldn't remember how he got the grass stains, but vaguely remembered taking a cab home with the two girls, who lived together in an apartment on College Street. He remembered the brunette attempting to kiss him and the blonde pawing at his crotch in a less than sexy manner, but him getting an erection anyway. He also remembered that at some point the cab pulled over and both of the girls had vomited in unison, just before they invited him back to their apartment for a "nightcap," which he thankfully declined.

When he got home around five a.m. Tamara and Noah were fast asleep. By the time he peeled himself out of bed and unceremoniously vomited in the bathroom sink, Tamara had gone to work and Amanda had taken Noah to school.

Charlie managed to finally leave the house and when he got into his office he discovered two messages on his voicemail. The first was from Ronnie, left around the time he was on his back in that field, staring at the stars.

"Never trust a girl with a butterfly tattoo, Charlie. Never. And don't fucking call me. Ever. Go ahead and have your fun. I don't give a fuck."

The second was from Sarah, left early that morning.

"I know what you're doing, Charlie, and I think it's disgusting. That girl. I saw the two of you arguing last night. You made a scene. And she's always coming to your office. I can hear the two of you. *I can hear you.* If you don't tell your wife I'll have to do it for you. Think of your child."

That was the problem, really. He was always thinking of Noah. Every moment of every day, Noah was the only reason for him to hold on to a life he really didn't want.

Things would be so much easier if he wasn't always thinking of Noah.

Things would be so much easier without Noah.

Charlie felt the bile from last night's whisky rise to his throat again.

CHAPTER THIRTY-ONE

"Well thanks to you it doesn't look like I'll be doing any university gigs any time soon."

Ronnie stared into her morning cup of Earl Grey tea while seated at the kitchen table. Her head was pounding mercilessly, and Ramona had nestled her head into her lap, looking up at her mournfully, sensing the disappointment in the room. Ronnie absently scratched behind the dog's ears, wishing Aaron would relent. "I'm really sorry. I think it was stress."

"Stress? Please." He refused to look at her. He was fully dressed to pick up things for a catering gig, while she had only just peeled herself from the bed after an evening of crying and apologizing. When they had returned from the party Aaron had been insistent that he didn't want to discuss what happened, and instead closed his eyes to sleep while Ronnie hovered above him, pleading for him to talk to her. Eventually she gave up and spent countless hours awake next to him before she finally drifted off.

"The party host informed me that while the food was great, I might want to look into how to better staff my events. I didn't even tell him that you're my wife."

Ronnie had noticed that Aaron had taken to calling her that lately, despite the fact that they weren't yet married and hadn't settled on a date. She knew this would be a bad time to correct him.

"I'm sorry. Again, I'm sorry," she said, absently rotating the diamond on her ring finger.

"And you know that money is tight for us right now."

"I know. I'll pick up more shifts."

"You have to ruin everything for us, don't you? Just because you're moody, or angry, or I don't know what. It's like dealing with a child."

"Fuck, Aaron. I said I was sorry. Can't we just drop it?"

"I love how you want to drop things when it's convenient for you."

Ramona reacted to the raised voices and slunk out of the room with her tail between her legs. Aaron barely noticed and continued his rant, his volume increasing.

"You're like this all the time now. I don't even know how to deal with you anymore. You know I try to be understanding. I try to accept that this is the way you are and the way you'll always be. But when you fuck up our chances like this?"

"Our chances? Our chances for what?"

"I don't know how exactly we're going to spend the rest of our lives together with you constantly sabotaging everything with your bad behaviour."

"Things aren't very good for me right now. You know that. I'm not well."

"Things are never good for you. It's always like this, whether or not you have a doctor's appointment. Honestly."

"Aaron. I'm not well."

"What the fuck is wrong with you, Ronnie?"

She of course didn't have a good answer to that question.

CHAPTER THIRTY-TWO

A few evenings later Ronnie called Charlie on his cellphone. She spoke before he even had a moment to say hello. "Charlie. Charlie. I miss you."

She called from a filthy bathroom at a bar on Bloor, where she stared at a piece of black-markered graffiti that said, "You're much better than you give yourself credit for." Ronnie never called Charlie late in the evenings—it was too dangerous—but she had had enough whisky shots to break this rule.

"Where are you?" he asked quietly.

She leaned up against the wall, watching the room tilt ever so slightly and things get fuzzy. "I know I'm not supposed to call . . . because of your wife . . . but I am at a bar by myself," she said quietly. "I am drinking and you are so close to me. I'm not angry, Charlie. I'm too tired to be angry. You are not far away. You should come watch me drink."

"Ronnie."

"Charlie. I don't think I can get home by myself."

"Don't move. I'll be right there. Okay?"

Even though they were still technically in an argument, even though she dropped a platter of cookies at his feet and threatened to bring out "the caterer," even though he had been pawed at by girls half his age and he remembered thinking, *Fuck Ronnie, she's not worth it*, he couldn't stop himself.

He told his half-sleeping wife that he was inspired and was going to the office to write. She moaned a response and barely stirred. He put on his parka, scarf, and boots and walked to the bar on Bloor

Street to watch Ronnie drink whisky shots in a shitty student bar with shitty students.

When he arrived he scanned the room and found she was seated at the bar by herself. She was wrapped in an oversized brown cardigan, her mascara smeared and her hair dishevelled. She threw her arms around him dramatically, clinging to him with a desperate surrender that made her body limp in his arms.

When she finally pulled away, she spoke without prompting, weeping while she did. "I don't care about the twenty-year-old girls you spend your time with. I don't care that you could have them all if you wanted. You're so smart and funny and famous it's no wonder they all want you—"

"Ronnie, stop it. It's not like that."

"But you are. You're smart and funny and famous and—"

"Shhhh. Honey."

Charlie rummaged in his pockets to find a Kleenex but came up with nothing. He grabbed some cocktail napkins from the other side of the bar and passed them to her. She blew her nose noisily and continued crying. "Considering what we're doing I can't judge you. How can I judge you? You can do whatever you want. All I care about is having you. I don't care how I have you. I don't care who else has you."

"There is no one else, Ronnie. There will never be anyone else." He cupped his hand on the back of her neck gently, resisting the urge to pull her in for a kiss. Despite the emotional display, they were still in public. It wasn't ridiculous to assume that one of his students could be sharing a ten-dollar pitcher a few tables over. Up until this point Ronnie could be disguised as an unstable student destroyed by a failing grade.

"Has there ever been anyone else? Ever?"

"No. Only Tamara. Up until now only Tamara."

With this knowledge, despite the fact that it was exactly what she wanted to hear, her eyes again filled with tears. "Oh god. I'm a terrible, terrible person. I should die. I deserve to die," she spluttered.

"Of course you're not. And no you don't. Don't talk like that."

"Do you think I act like a child? Do you think there's something wrong with me?"

"God no, Ronnie. You're perfect. Why would you even say that?"

Their conversation continued, and with slurred speech she talked about destiny and soulmates, and about her own mortality. She talked a lot about death. Charlie listened to her speak about a vague something that was wrong, saying nothing, just listening. What something she was talking about he failed to figure out entirely, no matter how hard he listened. Her words were a tangled, nonsensical mess as the whisky shots continued.

"Charlie, what are we going to do? What can we do?"

"There's nothing to be done. We'll just love each other, okay?"

"I'll be gone soon. When I'm gone, things will be easier."

"What do you mean?"

Ronnie didn't offer an answer. She hadn't told Charlie about the doctor's visits and the potential diagnosis, and despite her level of drunkenness had no plans to. When Charlie finally realized he would never figure out what she was talking about he drank some more whisky to help him understand, but things just got fuzzier and made less sense the more whisky he drank.

And then she told him, with certainty, that she loved him.

"I love you too, Ronnie. So much, I can't explain it."

Instead he explained the twenty-year-olds. Explained that they meant nothing and that he wanted only her. And after a few more whisky shots he explained he couldn't live without her.

I love you I love you I love you I love you I love you I love you

When the bar closed they were kicked out into the street, and they smoked and swore and went to his office and had sex on his desk. Because it was past three, Ronnie was encouraged to be as loud as she wanted and she was. They forgave each other by taking things out on each other.

"Will you really write a book for me?" she asked.

"Of course I will."

When they were finished, he asked her how she was, and she said nothing. She simply slipped on her clothes in silence and left him there, naked in a desk chair.

Charlie assumed nothing from her behaviour. He was simply pleased that they were speaking again. Even if they weren't actually speaking.

Charlie got dressed and slept on the couch in the office, the smell of her all over him.

(CHAPTER THIRTY-THREE)

"You know, Veronica, I know this really great fertility specialist that totally helped Aaron's sister-in-law. She had some of the same problems you're having, and she was even older than you are, and now she has twins. Can you believe it? Twins." Aaron's mother delivered this piece of information without making eye contact, wiping a non-existent crumb from the corner of her mouth with her white fabric napkin.

Ronnie did not make eye contact either, but instead watched as Aaron's father methodically carved a thin slice of roast beef from the great hunk of meat in the centre of the table, watched as the blood pooled in the bottom of the silver platter, unable to speak as Aaron's mother turned Sunday dinner into a critique of her fertility.

Aaron was visibly uncomfortable. "Mother, please. Not the time."

"Oh Aaron, honey. Sometimes women just need a little help. It used to be in my day that a woman really focused on getting pregnant. Took care of herself. But now it seems they just expect it to happen when they're busy with all these other distractions."

"Mother."

"Well, it's not as if I'm not saying anything that anyone at this table hasn't already considered," she offered, ignoring his protest. She adjusted the pearls around her neck, satisfied she was speaking for the good of everyone at the table.

"Actually, we haven't established whose problem it is yet," Ronnie finally said, not looking up from the roast beef even after Aaron's father had abandoned his carving and was refilling his wineglass.

"Oh dear, it's always the women. Never the men. And certainly not Aaron."

"Mother, stop it."

"No, Aaron. That's fine. I'm sure your semen is perfect," Ronnie conceded.

Aaron's father choked on his wine and descended into a coughing fit that lasted a good forty seconds.

"Veronica, I would appreciate it if you wouldn't discuss *those things* at the dinner table," Aaron's mother said disdainfully, returning to her napkin and the non-existent crumb.

"*Those things?* You mean Aaron's semen?"

"Veronica! Please. We're eating."

"Oh, I see. But my wasteland of a uterus is just fine dinner conversation? Well then, pass me some more roast beef so I can fuel up for this discussion of my barren womb." Ronnie reached toward the roast beef platter and plunged her fork into another hunk of meat, dramatically slapping it onto her plate, its juices splattering onto the white linen tablecloth.

Aaron reached over and put his hand on Ronnie's knee. "What's gotten into to you?" he asked quietly.

With this Ronnie stood up and tossed her napkin on the table. "Aaron, honey, if you need me I'll be in the car. Enjoy the rest of your dinner. Thank you for the advice."

"Oh god, Ronnie, please don't."

Ronnie grabbed the car keys from the front hall and ran into the driveway with Aaron trailing after her. She managed to get into the driver's seat and to lock all the doors of their Volvo station wagon before he approached.

"She didn't mean anything by it. She's just trying to help. Don't be like this. Please," he said through the glass.

"Just once. Just once, I'd love it if you actually defended me to them. Instead of being a fucking coward like you always are." She was crying now, the heat of her rage filling her face, her fists gripping the steering wheel as though she might take flight.

"I'm not a coward. I just don't see the point. They are the way they are. They're not going to change."

"The point is that you don't know how to be a man. A partner."

"Can we have this conversation inside? The whole neighbourhood is going to hear us."

"Oh god. Who cares if the neighbourhood hears us?" With this she leaned on the horn multiple times, numerous porch lights down the dark suburban street flickering on in reaction.

Aaron wandered away from the car, hands on his head while he paced the length of the driveway. Silence descended on the street, and Ronnie noticed that his parents had blown out the candles on the dining room table. She slowly rolled down the window, wiping the tears from her cheeks with the back of her sleeve.

"It's all too much. It's just too much," she said.

"I know, honey. I know."

He finally leaned in through the window and kissed her on the forehead in a way that suggested he understood.

"I guess we'll tell them we're getting married some other Sunday dinner," he said.

(CHAPTER THIRTY-FOUR)

Charlie and Ronnie met for their afternoon pint at a bar tucked away on a side street in the Annex. Afternoons were safer, simply because everyone in the world seemed to have something to do but them. Regardless of the locale, usually decided via email, they would meet up at the bar, their only witness a bartender with the unlucky privilege of working the low-tip daytime shift.

Ronnie arrived looking much like she usually did lately, tear-streaked, sullen, and puffy. Nonetheless, she smiled as she sat down at the barstool next to Charlie and ordered her first pint, and his anxiety was thankful for that smile. She touched the side of his arm tenderly, her expression suggesting he shouldn't ask what was wrong.

"It's so nice to see you," she offered.

She seemed to be crying more often now, but Charlie refused to pry. "How are you?" he asked, hoping for a lie.

"I'm okay. Now I'm okay," she said after taking the first sip.

She didn't want to taint their time together with her endless complaints, or accidentally reveal that Aaron had proposed. She knew she would have to tell Charlie eventually, that the ridiculous game of removing her ring and returning it to her finger when she left was growing tired, but for now she preferred the solace of him being unaware.

As the wedding plans unfolded with colour choices, expensive stationary, and elaborate menu items, Ronnie became increasingly withdrawn from Aaron and closer to Charlie. She was supposed to be fantasizing about her life with Aaron and instead she was wondering how she could escape it.

Aaron seemed blissfully, perhaps deliberately ignorant of the fact that Ronnie would cry quietly in the bathtub, when she was not touching herself and thinking of Charlie. There were occasions when she would touch herself and cry at the same time. And Aaron was oblivious to it all.

Charlie preferred not to think about what went on in the confines of Ronnie's west-end apartment, didn't want to know precisely why she was streaked with tears when she arrived. Her smile was so transparent at times, the kind of smile that failed to conceal the profound unhappiness that fell just below the surface. And although he longed to fix it for her, longed to assuage the frustration of constantly seeing her suffer, he instead smiled the same meek smile in her direction until they both had had enough wine, beer, or whisky to pretend that there was no "what went on."

And while his anxiety was thankful, his love made him wish that at least she would show up without the longing look of a girl with such profound loss, such profound unhappiness, the kind that is so boundless that feeling mediocre becomes a real goal.

Charlie wanted to believe he was the kind of man who could rescue a girl like Ronnie from her life, but he knew he could not. He would never be the hero. He was an overweight, sedentary ne'er-do-well, a man who couldn't support his family let alone manage the emotions of his mistress. So instead he provided her with a place where she could lie to him about her happiness until it was time to leave.

They exchanged pleasantries through the first pint, and then expressions of yearning through the second, and when the bartender turned away from them to polish glasses he put his hand on her knee.

"So, do you have anywhere you need to be this afternoon?" he asked.

"No. Only places I'm pretending to be," she said, smiling.

"My wife is at work and thinks I'm with students, and Noah is with Amanda at the museum, so I thought maybe you'd like to try something new."

"I didn't know there was anything new for us to try," she said and laughed.

"I thought you might be tired of the desk, so I got us a reservation at a hotel."

"Wow. Really? Are you sure it's my dislike of furniture that prompted this?"

"I just thought it would be nice. Romantic," he lied.

"Charlie. I don't believe you."

"You deserve better than a desk."

"That I'm sure of. But I'm also sure that's not why we're going to a hotel."

"Sarah called. She left a message. After the party. After the cookies."

"Of course. I hadn't thought of that. Aren't you worried about putting a hotel reservation on your credit card? That your wife will see it?"

"I'll pay cash." Charlie was a novice at this, but he'd seen enough movies to know exactly how the philanderer gets caught.

"So this is what it's like, then."

"What it's like?"

"An affair. I'd always wondered."

Ronnie poured back the remainder of her pint and took Charlie by the hand. "Let's go, then."

(CHAPTER THIRTY-FIVE)

It took over a month, but the news of Ronnie and Aaron's engagement finally began to spread among their friends and family. Aaron wanted to do a letterpress announcement card but Ronnie, with her quiet reservations, was resistant.

"We should get photos done. Engagement photos we can send to our parents," he said enthusiastically.

"But why?" she asked, genuinely perplexed as to why someone would subject their loved ones to posed glamour shots of them "in love."

Of course, when the news was discovered everyone was thrilled, and messages of congratulations crammed their mailbox, inboxes, and voicemail. There was, however, a degree of condescension to most of the well-wishes, each note suggesting "it's about fucking time," especially those that came from their families.

Ronnie's mother's immediate response, fuelled by white wine, was "Are you pregnant?" assuming that the couple could find no other reason to go the traditional route. To this query Ronnie laughed, although the entire idea of it depressed her more than ever.

"Really, I am very proud of you, sweetheart," her mother said.

"Proud of me for getting married?"

"Well, marrying someone like Aaron is something someone like you should be proud of, don't you think?"

As more people mailed and called in their well-wishes, Ronnie knew it was only a matter of time before she would have to tell Charlie that Aaron had proposed. Each time she saw him the words were in her mouth, but if they escaped she knew there would be endless tears and questions, and she was intent on living in the happiness of their meetings for as long as possible.

The proposal had the capacity to force a decision, what decision Ronnie had no idea, but she wasn't there yet. She wasn't ready to choose.

Aaron was forcing things as well, immediately interested in the complexities of wedding planning, and starting to fill a journal with his ideas, contacts, and to-do lists. Their apartment became a suffocating place of expectations, decisions, and fabric swatches. The possible-menu tastings were endless, their oven always on and full of things to serve to potential guests. Aaron had pooled all of his attentions into planning the perfect backyard wedding, as if perfecting the event was a way to distract from Ronnie's disinterest in getting married at all, which she was sure he was aware of. When Ronnie failed to care about making guest lists and ordering personalized coasters, he simply cut her out of it. "At the very least, find a dress to wear and show up. That's all I ask."

He pestered Ronnie to commit to a date almost immediately,

outlining the various virtues of spring, summer, and fall nuptials. During each conversation Ronnie found reasons to put off the event.

"What if I'm not well?" she finally said. The question felt strange as soon as she heard it, knowing that she, in fact, was not well. The tests so far had said as much.

"Don't be ridiculous."

"You never take this seriously."

"Of course I do. I just think you worry too much about things before they happen."

"Aaron, this is happening. It looks more and more like I'm going to have to get the surgery. You know that."

The surgery was easier to say than *cancer*. It was an event. Something that came and then went. Not an ongoing ordeal to be coped with.

"Fine. If that happens, it happens. But we can't put our lives off," Aaron said, not making eye contact.

"This is not us putting our lives off. This is our lives. This is my life."

Despite Ronnie's protests, they eventually decided on a June wedding, a little more that a year away.

"June is the only month worthy of us, no?" Aaron asked sincerely.

Ronnie laughed, but didn't explain why.

CHAPTER THIRTY-SIX

"You're going to marry him? And you waited until after to tell me?"

Ronnie was lying on her back in their king-sized hotel bed, having a cigarette in their non-smoking room. The blankets were looped around her midriff in a way that clothed her from the waist down. Charlie was propped up on one elbow, fully clothed.

"I've been trying to find a way to tell you. The time never seemed right."

"You know, Ronnie, you really shouldn't smoke. We might have to pay for that," Charlie said.

"It's adorable that you think me smoking in our hotel room is the biggest problem we're facing right now," Ronnie mocked.

Their trysts had been much more comfortable since Charlie had made the decision to stop meeting in his office. Although the hotel option was more costly and more difficult to conceal, it did prevent being heard or spotted by those hell-bent on exposing them. His writer-in-residence position had been winding down anyway, so their secrecy would become difficult. Charlie didn't regret this, he was glad the residency was coming to an end. He was more devoted to finishing the novel he had started, anyway, a book in which a version of Ronnie he had invented and defiled featured heavily.

As for new locales for their meetings, the Delta Chelsea would suffice. Rented for a day and used for only a few hours in the afternoon, the room would be empty and paid for overnight. Ronnie often suggested they give their key card to a homeless person upon leaving, while Charlie would suggest they meet again early in the morning for another romp. They generally did neither, as Charlie didn't trust the homeless and their mornings were generally reserved for guilt and remorse.

The first signs of spring had finally come to Toronto after a particularly brutal winter, and the thaw and smell of it caused Ronnie to feel somewhat more relaxed about balancing her affections for and liaisons with Charlie with the borderline platonic relationship she had developed with Aaron. While the intensity of her meetings with Charlie increased, at home she and Aaron barely touched each other, and Ronnie was struck by how unconcerned he seemed about this.

She still had an intense fear of being caught, of losing control over the surprise that she was not the good wife he hoped she would become, but she had to accept that she had come this far without getting discovered. Barring the occasional offhand comment from Lisa at the salon and the accusatory voicemail from Sarah, all evidence pointed to it being perfectly natural, even *preferable*, to have a domestic relationship with one man and a lustful, romantic tryst with another. One made the other tolerable.

In fact, she had become so comfortable with Charlie, everything became so familiar, that she could almost pretend she was in a relationship with him. When they had the rare opportunity to spend the night together, facilitated by some carefully constructed untruths (sleeping at Lisa's, working late at the office), they would brush their teeth together side by side in the mirror much like any married couple would. She enjoyed the simple details that affairs often avoided; watching him shave while she was seated on the toilet lid, helping him find his socks in the morning, reminding him of an afternoon dentist appointment and giving him a housewifely goodbye kiss at the hotel room door.

They chose to ignore the fact that the goodbye kiss at the door was merely a function of wanting to avoid being seen leaving a hotel together.

When they only had a few hours in the afternoon, Charlie always got dressed immediately after they had sex, while Ronnie tried to remain undressed and in bed until the final moment. Sometimes Charlie would get anxious and pace around the room aimlessly, checking his watch and then the red glow of the bedside alarm. She forgave him for this.

This time while Charlie paced his eyes were accusing her, the irony of his disdain escaping him. Ronnie took a long drag off her cigarette, looking relaxed and unaffected. "Let me get this straight. You're mad at me because I waited until after we fucked to tell you that I was going to marry him?"

"That's not the point, Ronnie."

"Answer the question."

"Yes. I'm mad."

"That's insane, Charlie."

"Why? I feel manipulated. Used. When did this happen?"

"Ha! You feel used?"

"Yes, I feel used."

"Charlie, you're using me a couple of times a week in a hotel room to get away from your wife. You're using me for your midlife crisis. You're using me to get laid."

"Stop it," Charlie said. "You know that's not true. But hell, if that's what you need to tell yourself to get by."

Charlie opened the minibar and pulled out a small bottle of Canadian Club. Ronnie smoked the final drag off her Belmont. They were silent as he poured the entire contents of the tiny bottle into one of the glasses on the dresser and drank a dramatic gulp.

"You don't want ice for that?" Ronnie asked.

"When did this happen?" Charlie asked, ignoring her.

"The proposal? A while ago. It happened a while ago."

"What the hell is a while ago?"

"About a month?"

"What the fuck, Veronica? You waited a whole month to tell me?"

"Actually, it's closer to two."

Charlie buried his head in his hands.

"God, don't be melodramatic. There's no need for that."

"Are you going to wear a white dress? Advertise your 'purity'?"

"God. What does that even mean?"

"It means you're a hypocrite. You had sex with me. Over and over and over and over and over," Charlie's volume had increased and he slammed down his glass hard on the heavy wood bedside table.

"You have some strange concepts of purity."

"All I know is that you fucked me knowing full well that you're planning on marrying him."

"And you fucked me knowing you're married. That seems worse to me. But it's not really a competition for who can be more inhuman, is it?"

"I'm just saying, having an affair while you're planning to marry someone is pretty sociopathic. Oh my god, are you planning a wedding? Are you planning a wedding in between seeing me? Are thinking about centrepieces when you're with me?"

Charlie had begun to pace around the room aimlessly, his fists clenched.

"Charlie, now you're being mean and slightly crazy. You need to calm down."

"Calm down? You're getting married."

"I didn't say I was planning on marrying him. I said that he'd asked me and that I said yes."

"Tricky, tricky," Charlie said, lifting his glass from the table and tipping it side to side mockingly.

Ronnie sat up, breasts exposed, her face a mixture of amusement, rage, and sadness. "Please. Couldn't you be upset that I'm going to marry him, instead?"

"I *am* upset about that. Does this mean you're leaving me?"

"Charlie, you're *married*. Have you left me yet?"

"You know, the day you tell me you're pregnant? That's the day I give up the faint hope that you'll ever leave him."

"I doubt there's much risk of that," she said, her face suddenly soft with sadness.

To this comment he finally relented. "Oh, Ronnie. I'm sorry."

He returned to the bed, whisky glass in hand, and ran his palm slowly and lightly across her shoulder, and when she sighed encouragingly, her left breast. He did so in a way that suggested he would miss her if she was gone. She smiled.

"Don't marry him, Veronica. Please don't marry him."

"Should I marry you instead?"

"You know that's not possible. You know it's complicated. You know I can't—"

"I deserve something. Something like what you have. A home. A life. A child. And besides, my marrying him will never change the way I feel about you."

Charlie sulked for a moment and then realized the gravity of her sentiment. "Because marriage means nothing to people like us," he said.

She knew that this was completely true.

"Is it awful that that makes me feel better about everything?" Ronnie asked sincerely.

Charlie put his glass on the bedside table, next to the makeshift ashtray, and leaned in to kiss her.

CHAPTER THIRTY-SEVEN

"Now, I totally understand cold feet and all that, but your lack of wedding excitement is starting to concern me. Most women would have gone intolerably loopy by now." Lisa put down her bottle of beer and continued applying dye to Ronnie's hair.

The shop was closed and the two had stayed late to have drinks and catch up. A few beers in, Lisa decided Ronnie should be a redhead and there was no convincing her otherwise. Ronnie had been too exhausted to object, a day of enduring the problems of her clients behind her and an evening of enduring her own ahead.

"I mean, aren't you supposed to be going crazy about dresses and flowers and all that by now? Aren't I supposed to be bored of you and all your wedding talk?"

"It's not that I'm not excited," Ronnie said, looking warily at her dye-soaked head in the mirror.

"It's just that you don't give a fuck."

"Yeah, that. Should you really be doing this drunk?" Ronnie asked, eyeing Lisa's exuberant application.

Lisa laughed. "You have no idea how many times I've done this drunk."

"I don't really want to know, thanks."

Lisa put the dye brush down and lit a Belmont. When Ronnie shot her a vague disapproving look for smoking in the salon, Lisa shrugged it off. "Honey, if you knew the shit I got up to in this place after hours you'd be thankful it was just a cigarette."

"I'm learning so much about you I never wanted to know," Ronnie replied.

"So why did you even say yes in the first place?"

"To Aaron or becoming a redhead?"

"To marriage, obviously."

"After a while you start to owe someone a commitment, no?"

"Uh, no. Fuck that. Life's too short for counting up who owes who what."

"Easy for you to say, you don't owe anyone anything."

"Yeah, but you owe me for this and how stunning you're going to be when I'm through with you. Men are going to be falling all over you."

"Like I need that in my life."

"Hey, do you think this hair dye causes cancer? 'Cause if so we're totally fucked, girl," Lisa said, her cigarette dangling from her lips.

(CHAPTER THIRTY-EIGHT)

"You changed your hair."

Ronnie touched her head self-consciously.

"I like it," Charlie said, pulling her in for a quick kiss without the fear that they would be spotted.

They had gone to a bookstore together that Thursday afternoon in May. Ronnie had driven them out to a big box store in Scarborough in the Volvo station wagon so they could be safe from being seen. They held hands as they walked through the door, and parted as soon as they were inside. The agreement that Ronnie had concocted was they would split up, find each other a gift—a book (not a yoga mat, or scented candle, or inspirational card)—and meet by the magazines when they were done.

Charlie hurried off to the children's literature section and Ronnie to health and self-help.

With their purchases tucked snugly under their arms and their fingers still entwined, they went for a pint at a faux-Irish pub on a suburban six-lane street to exchange their finds.

"Did you notice they only had four of my books there? A fucking crime."

"Charlie," she said, touching his arm lightly. "I need to talk to you about something important."

"I need to talk to you about something important! Four copies! Shameful."

"Listen to me. I've been trying to get you alone so I can talk to you about something important," she pleaded.

She realized how silly that statement was. They were always alone.

Charlie wasn't listening anyway. He had moved on to finding a typo in the menu. Typos on menus made Charlie crazy. Typos anywhere generally made Charlie crazy, misplaced modifiers and incorrect commas, but those on menus were a particular sore spot. He was visibly enraged and threatening to see the management while Ronnie tried to regain his attention. He was removing a felt-tip pen from his inside jacket pocket with the full intention of circling the improperly used apostrophe.

"Charlie, did you hear me? This is important. I had some tests done."

"What kind of tests? You know, it's not even as if they got it wrong. They actually made something up. They made a word up and put it in their fucking menu."

"A biopsy. I had a biopsy done."

Charlie finally looked up from the menu. He put the pen down on the table slowly. He stared at her and said nothing.

"It's really not a big deal. It's just a test. They found something they didn't like and they—"

Charlie's eyes suddenly welled up with tears. He gripped the old, heavy wooden table with such force that it shook, and then broke his own rule about touching in public by grabbing Ronnie's hand. "Why didn't you tell me?"

"I'm telling you now."

"There are so many things you never tell me."

"Charlie—" she said, pulling her hand away. "I'm sorry, Charlie. But this isn't really about you."

"You don't have cancer. You can't have cancer."

"I never said I had cancer. I just said—"

"Don't worry, Ronnie, you don't have cancer."

"I'm not worrying. I just wanted to tell you. It's early yet. We don't know what we're going to have to do." "What are we going to do? What are you and Aaron going to do?"

"No, what the doctors are going to do."

"What does that even fucking mean?"

"Surgery. Then I'll be better."

"But—the baby. You wanted a baby."

Ronnie had never heard Charlie refer to "the baby" before. "We still don't know anything."

Other patrons were staring now. Ronnie looked down at the various initials, hearts, arrows, and curse words engraved in the tabletop by suburban teens, bored and falling in love in Scarborough. She needed to avoid eye contact as Charlie stared at her with increasing intensity, so much that it unnerved her.

The waitress, ill timed, returned to the table with a second round of pints. She paused for a moment and stared at the menu and Charlie's felt-tip pen.

"Um, sir," she said when she put the pints down on the coasters. "You can't deface our menu." She put her French manicured finger directly on the apostrophe Charlie had circled.

"Fuck you," Charlie said.

The books lay out on the table, snug in their shopping bags, unopened, next to their untouched pints.

Charlie had bought Ronnie *Goodnight, Moon*.

Ronnie had bought Charlie a book on loved ones dealing with cancer.

She apologized to the waitress while Charlie found himself incapable of moving.

"I would have been able to give you a baby," he said.

(CHAPTER THIRTY-NINE)

The hotels, despite the expense, soon became ritual.

Charlie would invent imaginary literary events, occasionally pretending he was reading in a small town somewhere so he could spend the night. It amazed Ronnie that his wife never took the time to check, but he assured her that she cared little for the details of the literary world and wouldn't know where to look anyway. The only reason Ronnie believed it was because she wouldn't know where to look either.

As far as Aaron was concerned, Ronnie had seen her doctor,

her dentist, her chiropractor, her eye doctor, her massage therapist, gotten a pedicure (which Charlie did to maintain the ruse, painting her toes while she was nude), and developed a new passion for going to the gym.

"That's really great for the baby, Ronnie."

What baby? she thought.

The hundreds of dollars they spent on rooms was difficult to conceal, but somehow they managed it. It was exciting touring the city via its king-sized beds and room-service menus. Ronnie would always order the club sandwich, and Charlie would always drain the minibar of its Canadian Club.

They would often meet at the hotel instead of beforehand, and he would check in while she attempted to look inconspicuous from a distance, drinking a cocktail in the lobby bar to soothe her nerves or pretending to read Toronto tourism brochures provided by the concierge.

Ronnie had spent much of her adult life wondering longingly about the "anatomy of an affair," had seen it depicted in movies and on television in all its disastrous glory, but when she was actually in it it all seemed too easy. Calm. And certainly not glamorous. There was never anyone in the lobby to run into, no colleague, client, or old friend to spot them and question why they were there.

Still the nerves affected her. Once they had the key Ronnie would rush to the elevator, press the button rapidly, and fidget nervously until it arrived. If they rode it alone she would check for a camera as Charlie gripped her hips and kissed her. If they rode it with someone else Ronnie would stand as far away from Charlie as possible, even press the button for another floor to appear completely innocent. Once they got to the room she would close tight all the heavy curtains, claiming a perhaps faux concern that someone was spying through the windows in the opposite buildings.

She would turn on all the lights and turn up the radio, make things seems simple and inconspicuous, simply two colleagues chatting in a well-lit business travel hotel room. She would smooth flat the heavy garish blankets with her damp palm while Charlie washed his face in the bathroom sink.

Sometimes, as a treat, Charlie and Ronnie would have a steak dinner in the lobby restaurant of whatever hotel they were in. At first it was thirty-dollar steaks and then it was fifteen-dollar steaks, but it was always in the lobby because it was near impossible to comfortably have a steak dinner anywhere else. Ronnie got all twitchy and distracted with the fear that they would be spotted, and Charlie would make every effort to embarrass her to the wait staff. He would ask for "another cocktail for my little girl." And Ronnie would have another cocktail, and her head would be light and her resolution weak. Not that she ever needed excuses.

He would have his steak well done and she would order hers medium rare. They would talk about the university. They would talk about the clients she'd had that week. He would talk about his book. Eventually they made the rule that they would never talk about Tamara or Aaron, and if that rule was broken it would only lead to arguing.

They would certainly never talk about Noah, especially now that Noah was doing so much worse. Charlie would not mention the fact that he believed Noah was doing so much worse because he was never around.

They certainly did not mention cancer.

At first Charlie booked the Sheraton and the Westin, paid in cash, but as time wore on it was the Holiday Inn. Ronnie never questioned how he was paying the bill, always fearful that Tamara's billable hours were facilitating their affair. As the hotels got worse the water got harder and the conversations more strained, the curtains more musty, the fucking more frantic. Where at first it had been deep conversations and lovemaking, sweet and sticky like teenagers in those first months of discovery, they soon clawed at each other's bodies in a hungry desperation that suggested they were attempting to eradicate each other, that if they could only destroy each other the sinking weight of guilt would finally cease.

"Every moment I spend away from you is unbearable."

Generally when they would go back to their room, full of steak and vodka, they would make love first and then they would fuck, and Charlie would pin Ronnie down by her wrists and call her names, just like she asked him to. She asked him for all the things Aaron would never do. She would ask to be punished, and he would gladly oblige.

In so many ways she felt as if she was no one, and there was a private thrill of the fact that he picked her. He was a married man and as far as she knew he'd never picked anyone else. He picked her out of a room, out of a city, out of a world of people. A famous man picked a nobody like her—a girl who took her laundry to the laundromat and had to look up most of the words he used in the dictionary. Ronnie knew about all the countless wrongs of infidelity, the guilt that lingered in every moment they spent together, but there was something flattering about being chosen . . . she knew every moment he spent with her in that hotel room he was risking an entire life. A livelihood. The love of a wife and child. To be picked as a risk was an unbelievable compliment, and although she realized it wasn't exactly something to be proud of, his decision to see her did make her feel special. Beautiful.

Every time her hips bucked, the book he was penning in her honour became more pornographic. He wrote lines in his head during their most lustful moments, transcribing them into the manuscript until it was a stream of pointless scenes soaked with sweat and want, penned by a desperate man.

When they were finished he would lean in close to her ear and whisper the words "I love you," to which she wouldn't reply. Not that her reply mattered anyway. He would have loved her regardless of her response. He would cling to her tightly, their naked bodies sticky with sweat, and he would wait to hear a long sigh from her, an acknowledgement of her relief.

"Charlie, when you hold me it's like we're a pair of parentheses."

"What are we parenthesizing?"

"Is parenthesizing even a word?"

"Who cares?"

"You do, Charlie. You always care about words. You felt-pen typos on menus."

"And what do you care about?"

"You?"

"Us."

Sometimes she'd pull him down on the bed and she'd simply lean her head flat against his barrel chest and listen to him breathe. When he tried to pull her up to kiss him, she'd stop him, grip tightly to his frame and frantically hang on, and he would relent.

"What do you hear, Ronnie?"

"Something else."

Sometimes that was enough for her, the rise and fall of his breath just for her in a quiet room on a busy downtown street. Sometimes it didn't matter that he was married or that she would be. Sometimes she could justify a need for "other," that this was not a substitute but rather a supplement to a life that Aaron tried his best to fill.

Charlie would rotate her engagement around her ring finger while they lay together. "Why won't you take it off when we're together?" he asked her.

"Because I need to be reminded. It reminds me that this is worth it."

When they finally slept between the scratchy hotel sheets, safe in the knowledge that the people who waited for them at home believed them to be somewhere else, Ronnie dreamed of the desert. The sky blazed white and she ran barefoot through the sand, uphill, until the resistance became too much and she collapsed into its soft give. She lay still in the sand and gazed into the blinding light of the sky.

Charlie was the sky, and Aaron was the sand giving way beneath her feet.

When she opened her eyes, Charlie was snoring.

(CHAPTER FORTY)

"Have you ever had an affair?"

Ronnie and Lisa were having a beer on a patio on College Street post-shift on a Saturday afternoon. The day was warm and clear, the street busy with beautiful smiling people. Being out in it made Ronnie feel normal in a life that was feeling increasingly less so. After about three bottles Ronnie mustered the courage to test Lisa's moral compass.

"Fuck, yeah. Hasn't everyone?"

"Really? You're joking, right?"

Lisa took a long, thoughtful drag off her Belmont Mild and considered, her expression suggesting she was searching her personal history for examples.

"Can I have one of those?" Ronnie asked, gesturing toward the pack on the table between them.

"Since when do you smoke?"

"It's something I'm trying on. Please continue," Ronnie said, pulling a cigarette from Lisa's pack and lighting it with her friend's silver engraved Zippo.

"Well, yeah. Sure. Cheating. I mean nothing crazy invested or anything. But I've had a few too many gin and tonics and forgotten I was in a relationship. Dance floor antics. Alleyway gropings. That sort of thing. There was this one time I gave a—"

"I don't need details."

"All right, ya prude. Why do you ask?"

Ronnie stared out into the street, watching the tanned, scantily clad girls go by. There was a pause, and then a look of shock and sudden realization filled Lisa's face. Her voice fell to a hush. "Shit. Do you think Aaron's got something goin' on?" She looked around the patio as if to suggest they were being spied on.

"Oh god no. No way."

Lisa stared for a moment. A second realization snuck in. "Rons, are you saying what I think you're saying?"

"It . . . it just happened."

"What happened, exactly?"

"I met someone."

Lisa stared at Ronnie across the small table, concealing the lower half of her face with her half-full pint glass. Then she exploded, pointing her finger accusingly in Ronnie's direction. "I knew it! I fucking knew it!"

"What do you mean you knew it?"

"No, no, no. Wait. First things first. Please explain, you 'met someone'?" Lisa said very slowly.

"I mean that I met someone who is not Aaron."

"Jesus, Rons. I get that. Just who is this person? A client? Oh please say it was a client. I'd love that bit of gossip." Lisa's face revealed excitement. Maybe a tinge of self-satisfaction. Of "I saw this coming." Although it was hard to tell. Her facial expressions were often obscured by a degree of cosmetic theatrics.

"I met someone. And I don't know what I'm doing anymore. At first it was under control, but now I feel like I need to make some sort of decision."

"Oh, I'm loving this. And here I thought you were a good girl."

"Stop it."

"Again. I ask you, Veronica Kline . . . who is this person?"

"It doesn't matter."

"Fuck yeah, it matters. Whether or not I think you should leave Aaron is completely dependent on who this person is. Is he hot?"

"God, Lisa. You're without class sometimes."

"Class is overrated. Well is he?"

"Can you keep your voice down?" Ronnie glanced around the patio quickly to ensure there wasn't anyone relevant in earshot.

"Sorry. God. I would kill to have an affair."

"I think you have to be in a relationship to have an affair."

"Yeah, that too. Maybe I should, as they say, take a lover."

"C'mon, be serious."

"No, I really should. I'm bored out of my mind. You've got drama. Intrigue. Totally jealous."

"No, I've got serious problems. He's married."

"Shit."

"With a kid."

"Double shit."

"Who is sick." That word again. The one Charlie hated.

"My god, Ronnie. You must feel so lonely keeping this a secret. You should have said something."

This is why Ronnie loved Lisa. With all the people who flowed in an out of Ronnie's life, Lisa was the one who, despite being self-absorbed, genuinely cared about Ronnie's well-being above all else.

"Married with a kid, eh? So he's . . ."

"Yeah. He's older. You don't know him." Ronnie paused for a moment to reconsider. "Well, you might know him." Lisa was a reader, always carting around strange little books about feminism and novels by female writers Ronnie had never heard of. Ronnie was surprised that the literary fame factor hadn't occurred to her until this moment. "Charles Stern?"

"Wait a fucking second. You're fucking Charles Stern? *The* fucking Charles Stern? Literary god who has won a bunch of awards Charles Stern? You are fucking Charles fucking Stern?"

"Well, I wouldn't call him a god, per se."

"Shit. I can't even believe this. The injustice of it. You don't even care about books. How do you get to fuck Charles Stern?"

"That's not true. I read books."

"Yeah? What was the last book you read?"

"That's not the point."

"My god, you always seemed so Ivory soap and water, or bread and butter, or whatever that phrase is to imply you're a good girl. Wonder Bread? Whatever. Fuck you."

"Thank you."

"Oh my god. You're fucking Charles Stern."

"Would you stop. Please."

"What about the wedding? Your wedding?" Lisa said this in a tone that implied she'd entirely forgotten about the wedding. There were times when Ronnie herself forgot the wedding.

"I'm starting to think I'm not really cut out to be a wife. I'm not the baking pies and knitting sweaters type."

"No one is. That's why there are bakeries and malls. Get over it."

"Again, not really the point."

"So, what are you going to do?"

"I have no idea. Drink this beer?"

"Hell, drink ten beers. I'm buying. Honey, you're fucking Charles W. Stern."

(CHAPTER FORTY-ONE)

Ronnie decided to cut hair because she didn't know what else to do. She'd simply never had any real interest in anything, no passion or calling, and the idea that as a hairdresser she could work flexibly and independently appealed. It was also easy to learn and do while she was being reckless or sick. Or both.

She'd never been the kind of girl who was preoccupied with fashion or beauty, but her ability to make people feel good, happy, and attractive was immediately gratifying. It fit. It was easy. The feeling that she could fix something, make something better with a skill she had acquired, that people trusted her, told her their secrets, relied on her to symbolically overhaul their lives—all of these things made the profession a perfect place for her to be.

It was for this reason that she asked Charlie if she could cut his hair. Her feelings for him, for the situation, had lost their footing, escaped reason. The floor was falling out from beneath them. Cutting grounded her. Brought her clarity. It was a way to save them both.

"But I have so little hair to cut," he said, half smiling.

"I want to do it. I've sat here and watched you write."

Here was an ever-changing hotel room. Home, for them, was club sandwiches from room service and white towels and concierge requests.

"I want to share what I do with you," she pleaded.

He smiled at her, soothed by her simplicity, and relented. "I want you to."

This particular excuse to be missing for an afternoon was an easy one. "I'm going to get a haircut," he told Tamara.

Ronnie laid a bath towel down on the floor, and after he came from the shower in a complimentary bathrobe, she slipped her scissors and combs from her backpack and placed them neatly on the bed. Charlie sat in an office chair facing the mirror, over the desk, next to a window with an endless view of the city.

She put her hands in his hair and then put one on each of his shoulders.

She stared at him seriously in the mirror. "I love you, Charlie."

"I know you do."

"Do you trust me?"

"Always."

"I want you to leave your wife."

"I know you do."

They hadn't spoken about her tests, the possibility of cancer, the possibility of surgery, since the crying jag at the pub. Ronnie had decided not to push Charlie to deal with reality until it was indeed reality. When she had results, when she had a plan, she would bring him in, but for now she wanted to protect him. To care for him. To hide it all from him.

They were silent for a moment, and when it was obvious that Charlie was going to say no more, she slowly ran her fingers along one side of his neck. He closed his eyes and let out a long, low sigh.

When he opened them again he nodded and she began cutting, carefully at first, and then with an intensity and speed that suggested she was lost in it.

She worked in silence, and he watched her in the mirror, her furrowed brow, the flicker of her eyes as she scanned and then confirmed each cut, soothed by the knowledge that when they went down, they would go down together.

And in that moment everything that was out of control wasn't anymore.

(CHAPTER FORTY-TWO)

Fidelity becomes infidelity so quickly.
One touch becomes another. One word becomes another.
Safe becomes unsafe so quickly.

Pre-cancerous becomes cancerous so quickly.
One test becomes another. One treatment becomes another.
Safe becomes unsafe so quickly.

You nod through conversations about outcomes and expectations, and you know you can't have your lover care for you in a hospital bed. It's simply not practical. Despite the fact that you love him more than anyone else in the world, that he is the subject of songs and movies and visits you in dreams, that you smell your clothes in the hopes of catching the scent of him on them, that you have given your heart and soul to him in hotel rooms across the city on a weekly, almost daily basis, have suffered every risk and regret, perpetuated every lie to have him in your life, it's difficult to explain the stranger at the foot of your bed, doting on you, as you lose weight and your hair falls from your head and your eyes sink back into your skull.

If you're honest, you know how little this narrative means in the greater scheme. While your love is scandal, and has the capacity to wound so many, it's all so meaningless. Your lives so small and insignificant. People tell lies and betray the people they love every day. Your mistake is thinking you are somehow special in this regard. You're simply two extra people groping to find meaning where there is little to none.

The beauty of infidelity is that you love so quickly. There is nothing to lose in confessing the enormity of your love.

Everything is already lost.

(CHAPTER FORTY-THREE)

Ronnie was at the meat counter in the supermarket and something made her cry. Made her wonder if she was being punished for what she had done in hotel rooms and steakhouses, at university cocktail parties, in Bay Street bars.

Surrounded by endless cuts of meat, flesh segmented, carved up, shrink-wrapped and frozen, sliced and served on Styrofoam, all the parts of her that had been poked and prodded, all the parts that had been cut up and put in tiny plastic jars, labelled *Veronica Kline*, to be sent off to labs. The parts they had burned off. The parts that were discarded.

At the meat counter, she started to cry. She cried for the time she had shamefully bled all over the floor of the hospital room, and the nurse, sympathetic, handed her a maxi-pad and her jeans. She cried for the many med students who hovered above her, with their clipboards and busy questions, their vague interest and vaguer statements, their endless chorus of "we don't know anything yet." She cried for the time a male med student, likely ten years younger than her, said, "I know how you feel," when he clearly didn't and never could. She cried for the time the doctor threatened to put her out, put her under, if she didn't "calm down." She cried for the time she had cried from the moment she lay down on the table until well after they were finished. It always took so long for them to be finished. Took them so long to slice out the parts that they wanted and take them away for safekeeping. She cried for every question unanswered and every test inconclusive.

She remembered the time she cried when Charlie fucked her. The time she cried when Aaron fucked her. And how the two times were so different. How they both let her cry and didn't ask any questions.

She remembered the time she left the house and went to a dive bar by herself in the middle of the night and drank half a dozen whisky shots and had to have Aaron come to get her. The time she wished she could have called Charlie instead. But Charlie was with his wife at a dinner party, and Charlie's wife didn't have cancer. Charlie's wife was beautiful and not sick and not spending her afternoons being carved up on a gynecologist's table.

Ronnie was at the meat counter and she wondered how, when the time finally came, she was going to tell Aaron that she couldn't have children. When the doctor called to tell her surgery was the only option, how she could look Aaron in the face and explain that she could never give him what he really wanted. She wondered if that would be a good enough reason for him to leave her, because she longed for him to leave her. Longed for the relief that would finally bring. She of course could never leave him. He was beautiful and good and perfect and everyone loved him. She would never be able to explain.

Surrounded by cuts of meat, seeping, bleeding onto their Styrofoam trays, Ronnie cried for a baby she didn't want, and a husband she didn't want, and someone else's husband that she did want.

The butcher wiped his hands on his apron and asked her if she was okay.

"He's never going to leave her," she said to the butcher with the clean hands.

(CHAPTER FORTY-FOUR)

Despite the fact that Charlie and Ronnie had moved their meetings to various hotel rooms across the city, far from the heavy, creaking wooden desk of his University of Toronto office, Sarah still had her suspicions and was bored enough with her own life to pursue them with calculated interest.

She decided to invite Tamara and Charlie to a dinner party at her home one Friday evening. There were other guests, various writers and professors picked at random, merely characters in the play she sought to direct, the one where Charlie slipped up and Sarah could publicly reveal his indiscretions.

It was for this reason Charlie was reluctant to attend, but Tamara was excited to socialize with colleagues of his she hadn't met. "I like being part of your work," she said, smiling affectionately.

Charlie cringed at this, feeling she was clinging to an act they were no longer any good at. "But these people are so boring."

"Please, Charlie. I never get to hang out with adults. I'm always with Noah."

Generally Charlie would have been terrified by a scenario like this, given Sarah's accusatory phone call and her consistent penchant for meddling, but lately he felt a lack of concern as he openly sent emails and took phone calls from Ronnie at his end of the couch.

As Tamara got dressed that evening, carefully doing her make-up and hair in the upstairs bathroom, Charlie was reminded of how beautiful she was, remembered how in those early days together she was the most stunning girl he had ever seen. How he had been amazed that for even one moment she had wanted him that night at the campus bar, that she had taken care of him, taken pride in being the writer's understanding girlfriend.

"I imagine I'll write a whole book."

As he watched her run a brush through her hair he realized he had never written that book he promised her, wondered how things had so unravelled, how he had forgotten to look at her this way. The love he felt for her was deep in his bones, the kind that never goes away no matter how many hours are spent with someone else in a paid-for room.

"You look lovely," he said from the doorway.

She half-smiled in a way reserved for insecure girls. "Thank you, Charlie."

They left Noah at home with Amanda and barely spoke on the cab ride over to Sarah's apartment. Their weeks of bitter awkwardness and resentment had descended into silence, both of them deciding that it was simply better not to speak than to inevitably get into an argument.

Regardless, when they arrived for dinner, Tamara fell easily into her old role of the comically patronizing writer's wife, a routine the academics and their wives and husbands greeted with consistent wine-soaked laughter.

"Charlie wouldn't know how to drive a car let alone fix one," Tamara said lightly as Sarah refilled her wineglass.

"I imagine the poet mechanic could be a lucrative gig, Charlie," one dinner companion offered. "You should really look into it if the old writing gambit doesn't pay off."

He smiled at the painfully awful jab, realizing his writing was a gambit that didn't pay much of anything.

"So Tamara, what do you do with yourself while your husband is gallivanting around?" Sarah asked abruptly.

"I keep busy. Although it has been hard with him doing all these events lately."

"Events? Really? Charlie, you hadn't mentioned."

He shifted, uncomfortable for a moment. "Nothing special, just the usual," he said, searching his mind for a lie.

Tamara thankfully interjected. "Such is the life of a writer's wife, I suppose. You know what you sign up for," she said, giving her most sparkling smile. Another guest offered a toast to writer's wives and husbands, and everyone but Sarah smilingly raised a glass.

For the rest of the meal—largely jovial with light conversation and a few too many drinks—Sarah stared severely at Charlie from across the table, trying desperately and unsuccessfully to find a chink in his armour. To everyone else Tamara and Charlie were the perfect couple; him the bumbling genius and her his devoted caretaker.

The evening wound down and Sarah called Charlie and Tamara a cab, lingering with them in the front hall as they put on their shoes and waited for it to arrive.

"It was really nice to see you, Charlie," Sarah said. "Considering we don't see much of you at the university anymore. I know you're really missed by the students."

Tamara looked genuinely confused. "But I thought you were spending a lot of time with them lately?"

There was a moment of brief discomfort, and Sarah assumed she had finally found an opportunity to provoke a confession, but with Charlie the lies never ceased. "Indeed I am. Mostly off-site though. It gets a bit oppressive at the university. The students work better where they feel comfortable."

Tamara smiled. "See? I knew you'd be great at this, Charlie." She kissed him lightly on the cheek, a gesture that warmed him and made him temporarily forget that he had fallen in love with anyone but her.

The cab arrived and they sat quietly in the back as it drove them home. Tamara casually unclipped her long wavy hair from its shiny French twist and let it fall to her shoulders. She turned to Charlie slowly, staring at him in silent adoration for a few moments.

"You know, Charlie, you're a wonderful father. Please don't ever forget that."

He was thankful she had said it, needing the reminder in the mess he had created.

"It's just that I miss this. I miss you," she said, placing her hand on his knee.

Charlie waited for the guilt but it never came.

"Me too," he said, squeezing her hand.

CHAPTER FORTY-FIVE

Ronnie didn't know what the word ennui meant before she met Charlie. More importantly, she didn't know she was experiencing it before she met Charlie.

One day at the salon a teenage boy in a Smiths T-shirt and a pair of scuffed Converse All-Stars came in for a cut. His hair was long and soft, the kind of hair that teenage boys have because they fail to wash it regularly and never style it. It was light and feathery and beautiful, a sort of non-colour, a uniform grey-brown. He collapsed heavily in her chair and she found herself running her fingers through it lovingly, carefully concealing this love from him as he stared severely at her in the mirror.

"Is there something wrong with you?" was the first thing he said. The question shook her from wherever she was.

"What do you mean?" she said, pulling her fingers quickly from his scalp.

"You don't look well. You look sick."

In trying to avert his gaze Ronnie noticed his face, naïve yet knowing. Perfect.

"No. I'm fine. What are we doing today?"

"Cut it all off," he replied emphatically.

Ronnie's eyes widened. She couldn't bear the thought of cutting off his hair. It was beautiful. There was a myth she couldn't remember, maybe a Bible story, about hair and power, this beautiful boy with his beautiful, powerful hair she couldn't bear to cut off.

Cutting hair had become increasingly difficult while the doctors were cutting at her. She couldn't suffer the loss of anything else. And his hair between her fingers was perfect and worthy of being saved.

"Are you sure?" she said, lifting her scissors dramatically from her belt.

"I need you to cut her out of it. I hate her."

Only teenagers can get away with saying things like that to strangers.

He was heartbroken. Of course. She should have known. His misery and beauty, his suffering palpable. People who were heartbroken always had that same distinguishing glow, as if they were about to simultaneously hug and destroy everything around them.

Ronnie uncharacteristically put her hand on his shoulder. "You don't need to do that. I'm sure it's not that bad."

"She kissed my best friend."

Ronnie almost laughed at this; the idea that a kiss could bring this boy so much despair, considering all of the perverse, secret things she'd done. She stifled the impulse, nodding seriously, empathetically.

"Please. Just cut."

There was a pause, an acknowledgement, and without further question Ronnie cut. The feel of his hair falling around her fingers was exquisite. His miserable, accusing stare exquisite.

After many minutes of silence between them, while Ronnie was working, the boy finally spoke. "Why would someone do that to someone else? Betray them like that?"

The question was actually one she'd had many hours to ponder, so she answered quickly. "Maybe because they need something else. Something different. Something more."

"But I gave her everything she could ever want."

"Nobody can give someone else everything they want," Ronnie said coldly, focusing on cutting.

"Then what's the point? If you can't give someone everything, then why bother trying to be in a relationship? Why bother trying to be in a relationship with anyone?"

"I think you just need to find someone who is happy enough with 'almost enough.'"

"Someone who wants mediocre?"

"Yeah, there's tons of those people. They're everywhere. Go ahead and let the people who aren't satisfied destroy each other with their wanting."

She couldn't believe she was saying all this to a seventeen-year-old boy. Regardless, he seemed pleased.

"No one's ever said that to me before. Everyone always says you'll find someone who's right for you eventually."

"Well, everyone is wrong. Or lying."

The hair fell from his head and floated around them like confetti. With each cut the boy's face became exponentially more beautiful. He became lighter.

"Thanks for not lying to me. You're the only person who hasn't lied to me. You're the only person who hasn't told me that everything is going to be okay."

"Because it's not going to be okay. But it's going to be beautiful anyway."

The boy's hair was gone. She ran her palm across his soft, round head and sighed dramatically, watching his eyes fill with tears.

"I really loved her, you know."

There was nothing she could say, though he didn't really expect anything further. He tipped her five dollars and skulked off the chair, his scuffed sneakers stepping into the pile of hair that surrounded them.

CHAPTER FORTY-SIX

"You understand what this means, Veronica?"

"It means I'm dying?"

"No, sweetheart, we're far from that. We're so far from that."

Ronnie's doctor always called her sweetheart. Being called sweetheart by someone in rubber gloves was almost intolerable. Receiving sweetness from someone who only ever touched you with a thin film of latex between you and them was disingenuous.

"I was kidding."

"What a strange sense of humour you have."

"Well, what does it mean, then?"

It meant another day, another biopsy. It meant more tests. It meant cancer, that word that had been rattling around in her head for months, for years. It meant, inevitably, surgery. It meant hysterectomy.

From the Greek, hystera, meaning "womb."

From the Greek, ektomia, meaning "a cutting out of."

The surgical removal of the uterus.

May be total or partial.

Removal renders the patient unable to bear children.

A cutting out of.

The parts that were discarded.

At the age of thirty-five. It means telling Aaron they'll never have a baby.

It means being disappointing. Failing again.

They had carved so much out of her cervix in the last year she was surprised there was anything left of it.

"It could mean more treatment. Or it could mean surgery. Either way, we're going to do our very best to ensure you get the best care."

Despite the reassurances, Ronnie was clear on the metaphor; a woman so unsure of her ability to be good at being a woman gets the part of her that makes her a woman removed.

Can't get pregnant, can't bake a casserole, can't have a uterus.

The thing that surprised Ronnie was that regardless of how much they cut and craved and burned away, her lust never left her. Despite the fact that she had parted her thighs repeatedly for cold metal instruments beneath the flicker of fluorescents, that she had felt the scrape and cramp of every invasive test, she still longed for Charlie inside her. His fingers, his tongue. She felt as if he had a capacity to heal her, that he could blot out all the damage with fingertips and mouth, that he could swallow the cancer, will it away with his hot breath. Even when she was sore from procedures, even when they told her that sex was out of the question.

When it came to the reality of what would certainly be surgery, Charlie was falling apart more than she was. He tried to hold it close, but his grief spilled out of him in bars, restaurants, and hotel rooms. Ronnie would hold him tight to her while he cried, their naked limbs tangled up, clinging in their desperation. There were great stretches where Charlie had the ability to pretend things would be okay. His anxiety had given way to despair and he had accepted it readily. Despair was so much easier to tolerate than anxiety. The depression was a welcome wave, flattening the edges of neurosis out so his relationship with the world became fuzzy at best.

"Love grows in me like a tumour, Charlie."

"Stop that. Stop. Stop. Stop. What an awful thing to say," he would cry, clasping his hand over his ears like a petulant child.

"I was kidding."

"You need to stop kidding. And smoking. I hate watching you

smoke. I just think about you dying. You need to eat better. No more steaks. No more martinis."

"How optimistic of you, Charlie. Way to be a trooper."

"Do you always have to make a fucking joke? This is serious."

"What else am I supposed to do? Lie down and die?" Ronnie lit another cigarette from the one she was smoking, just to spite him.

Charlie couldn't go to the hospital with Ronnie, and this fact alone destroyed him. He wanted to hold her hand while they took tiny pieces of her and put them in tiny vials with her name scrawled on them to be sent to be tested. He wanted to be there when they finally cut her open. But that was Aaron's job, and Aaron was stoic. Aaron was good at that sort of thing. He was the kind of boy you took home to your mother when you wanted to prove to her that you hadn't fucked up your life. Charlie was fucking up both of their lives and loving it. Charlie was too far gone and Ronnie knew it.

"Charlie, do you ever think that we are home wreckers?"

"There has to be a home to wreck for that, doesn't there?"

"You have a home. You have a home with Noah."

"Some days I'm not entirely convinced that Noah knows who I am."

(CHAPTER FORTY-SEVEN)

Ronnie began lying about things she didn't even need to lie about.

She'd lie about what she had for lunch.

She'd lie about the movie she watched.

She'd lie about her clients at work.

She became so skilled at it that each lie she uttered fell out easily, unquestioned.

She pushed and pushed and pushed at Aaron, her deception everywhere, waiting for it to click in his brain. But it never did.

And because Aaron never asked any questions, never rummaged through her things, never called to check up on her, Ronnie grew to loathe him. The fact that she was having an affair and Aaron had no suspicions made her feel like he didn't care, and in turn his lack of care became a good way for her to justify the affair.

"The fact that he doesn't seem to notice just proves that he doesn't really love you," Charlie said during one of their weekday pints.

"Has Tamara noticed?"

"That's different. Married people are different. Things become comfortable and you don't worry anymore." Charlie knew this was a lie, given that Tamara had expressed that she missed him regardless of not actually knowing where he had gone.

"So your reasoning is that Tamara loves you because she's complacent?"

"No. She trusts me. It's almost twenty years of trust."

"That certainly doesn't make me feel any better about what we're doing, Charlie."

"What we're doing is necessary. I'm happy when I'm with you. I'm alive when I'm with you. I need to be with you."

"God, you can be so dramatic."

"Well, it's true."

"You just need attention. That's why you surround yourself with pretty young things."

"Listen, Ronnie, you're not some dewy-eyed undergrad who's cooing at me that she loves my work. Have you even read my work?"

"Will you be angry if I say no?"

"Of course not. I love you because you haven't. I find it refreshing. I find it real. You're real."

Ronnie laughed.

"What are you laughing at?"

"You," she answered. "You're . . . I don't know."

"In love?"

"Yes. That."

Charlie and Ronnie would send each other messages, inventing more and more ways to see each other. Events and dinners, everything clandestine, everything far enough off the grid that they wouldn't get caught. His email account full, her phone messages deleted.

For Ronnie, there were great, fleeting moments of clarity. She would see herself leaving Aaron—filmic moments that involved her running through a cool evening without a coat, running to Charlie's front door, exclaiming, "I've left him." And always Charlie would be pleased. He would pull her inside and kiss her hard on the mouth, pulling her clothes from her body right there in the front hall, groping at her like an impatient child.

And caught in all this wanting, Ronnie made a list, written out on a steno pad in the early evening while Aaron was at the gym, while the dog lay at her feet, dreaming of chasing animals through the park.

She made a list of things she'd couldn't do with Charlie. Things she longed to do, rendered impossible by their situation. Things that she dreamed of doing daily, things she fantasized about while twisting her engagement ring around the finger of her left hand, hoping secretly for a random tragedy to make things hard, to make things easier.

1. Read the Sunday paper with you
2. Kiss you in a bar populated by our friends
3. Have you take care of me when I'm sick
4. Take care of you when you're sick
5. Listen to you tell someone you love me
6. Tell someone I love you
7. Slow dance
8. Make breakfast together
9. Do laundry together
10. Hold hands walking down the street
11. Bring you as my date to a wedding
12. Kiss you at midnight on New Year's
13. Try to figure out what to watch on TV
14. Fight with you about domestic duties
15. Have you walk my dog
16. Put new sheets on a bed together
17. Nap in the afternoon while it's raining
18. Celebrate your birthday with you
19. Meet your parents
20. Wake up together on Christmas morning

After scrawling out the list, she rewrote it with careful penmanship on a piece of crisp stationary. One day she worked up the courage to give him this list at another Bay Street bar.

He read it thoughtfully, in silence.

When the empties of their first round were collected, Charlie told the bartender he loved Ronnie.

CHAPTER FORTY-EIGHT

In the bathtub one evening, submerged beneath bubbles and feeling all too tired, her hair floating like a halo around her, Ronnie finally realized what was wrong with her and Aaron. Why she felt the urge to fill her voids, to lie, to hide away, to hide from him. She plunged forcefully upright, through the surface of the water, the force of the realization like a sudden fist.

Aaron didn't need her.

She sat up in the bathtub, realizing Aaron of course loved her, but he would never, ever need her. He was together and practical and naturally took care of everyone around him.

Aaron was the type of person who would clearly never need anyone.

Charlie needed Ronnie. She knew that when his head was resting in her lap, when she smoothed her fingers through his hair, searching for greys, finding and examining them, and never telling him. She would touch him and he would close his eyes and sigh noisily, groping for her hand and squeezing it tightly when he found it. The force of his hand on hers, the desperate clutch of a man in need, was enough to convince her. Ronnie knew Charlie needed her because he would answer her call in the middle of the night. He would come when she called.

She knew Charlie needed her because his face twisted into a look of pain when she pulled away. Like he was personally wounded that she had somewhere else she needed to be, someone else she needed to be with. When the guilt of what they were doing rose in her throat, Charlie would do everything to convince her to stay, that there was nothing wrong, regardless of how untrue that was.

He would press her tightly to him like a vice and tell her how he longed to see her happy, that she deserved to be happy. That he could make her happy. He would fight to prevent her from putting her clothes back on, his hands slowly traversing the map of her back, that closed-eye sigh returning.

She knew Charlie needed her because he would tell her any lie to get her to stay. She could see the lies in his face, the way he chose to make up reasons why what they did was not wrong, if only to see her slip the clothes from her body and have her curl up next to him. Charlie needed her because when she curled up naked beside him in whatever hotel bed they were in that week, he would make promises he couldn't and wouldn't ever keep.

She knew Charlie needed her because he would do everything in his power to pretend that the real world failed to exist when they were alone together. And she knew she needed him back because she would allow herself to believe him.

That was need.

So, in the name of need, Ronnie stepped out of the bathtub and ran out of the bathroom—naked, dripping wet—and into the bedroom, her feet leaving wet footprints down the hall. The dog looked up at her from a snug, tightly curled ball on the bed, sensing her sudden urgency as Ronnie quickly pulled her clothes on, still soaking, soaking through her blue jeans and T-shirt, her hair matted against her face in damp webs. The dog, assuming a walk, followed her, watched as she rummaged in the hall closet to grab a coat, and stared as she escaped out the front door and into the street.

It was raining.

Every fantasy she had about Charlie and her finally being safe together involved the rain. It was always raining in her head when she decided to leave Aaron.

Aaron didn't need her. Ronnie wanted only to be needed.

Through the rain Ronnie ran to catch the streetcar, paid with quarters, and walked to the back of the car, soaked through. The other passengers stared, the rain dripping from her lashes, her forehead, her fingers onto the floor. She suffered the endless ride down Queen West, to Spadina, onto another car heading north. She pushed through the doors before they were fully open, and peeled off the car into the street.

Maybe Ronnie was bad and maybe that was enough. Maybe she needed Aaron to take care of her, fix her, fight her battles for her, make her better.

All of these things that I have done.

But maybe she needed Charlie to need her. Maybe she needed Charlie to mark up menus and lament cancer and say inappropriate things to waiters. Maybe she didn't need someone to be strong for her, to fix the pieces of her that were supposedly broken, to help her pull through. Maybe she could try to do that for herself. Maybe instead she simply needed someone like Charlie to fall apart at the mere thought of losing her, to mindlessly finger the graffiti on the table at the thought of biopsies, to outline aimlessly the bursting arrowed hearts of other people's love carved into tabletops, to misguidedly correct the typos in the menu, to tell the bartender he loved her, to bring her back from the brink, to vice grip her into believing she'd done nothing wrong, to touch her in every moment they were together, incapable of not being connected to her when she was in sight, afraid of the excruciating possibility that they would be parted, wounded by the table between them when the were in public, kissing her in empty elevators, in the back of a bookstore, in a deserted restaurant . . .

Turning a corner, running through the rain. Still decidedly aimless. Careless.

Reckless.

Maybe she needed Charlie to tell her that her bad was enough for her.

More than enough for her.

Always enough for her.

Nothing to fix and nothing to mend.

That her brokenness was something beloved.

That it was enough. To be needed. That being needed was more than enough.

She ran down Charlie's street. The rain blinded her, made her temporarily unsure of where his house was. After he finally told her where he lived, she would sometimes request that cab drivers take her on a route past his house if only to get a glimpse of it. She remembered the red door with the brass knocker. The crooked mailbox and the maple in the front yard. Up to the front path and to the door. She eyed a few of Noah's toys strewn across the front lawn: a red wagon, a soccer ball, a basketball hoop. Ronnie lifted her fist to knock and froze.

She felt so old. She felt that she had missed everything, that as she got older she had tried so hard to be good that she had forgotten herself. She longed for her youth, the sweet misery of being young and misguided, the sweet taste of blood in her mouth in the morning after she had destroyed everything, not knowing where the blood had come from, not knowing the source of the wound, the bile of the mistake, the guilt and regret of all those flawed choices. And never caring. She missed never caring.

With her fist raised; she knew that this moment would obliterate everything. That the earth would be burned and the building would collapse and the world as they knew it would shift into an orbit unknown. The fire around her was about to spread to the house, and with her fist raised she knew she would ignite the failure of ten years, twenty years of work. That when her fist hit his front door, on his charming Annex house that he lived in with his wife and his "special needs" child, where he wrote his books and wondered about his reviews and admirers, where he jerked off in the shower over thoughts of her, where he kept her photo in the bottom of a desk drawer, where he called her quietly from his cellphone in the middle of the night.

The fire was destined to spread, and as she knocked she felt the ignition.

She heard feet in the hall, light and quick, too light and quick to be Charlie's, and the fear of Tamara opening the door rocked through her immediately. The doorknob turned and the door swung open.

Noah.

"Pretty," he said, blinking up at her, his small, thick finger pointed upward.

(CHAPTER FORTY-NINE)

"I'm leaving him. I left him."

But how did you actually leave?

Did you pack a small bag and leave a small note? Or did he watch you pack every last item, right down to a box of condoms and your best pair of underwear?

Did you argue about that Stone Roses record? About whose copy of *Ulysses* that was, a copy of *Ulysses* that neither of you had ever read? Did you divide up the cutlery drawer evenly and fairly? A ladle for you and a spatula for him?

Did you open the conversation by saying "we have to talk"? And when you did, did his face drop and his smile fade?

Was there crying?

Did you hold him?

Did you fuck him a final time, in a rabid, hateful way that sealed your fate? Knowing that being alone was better than being crowded and smothered by pervasive apathy?

Or did you cut and run and start again in an empty room? How did you find that empty room? Did you covertly search the want ads for hours while he was sleeping? One bedrooms and studios all over the city, waiting for your small bag and semi-broken heart? Did you tell a trusted friend who loaned a couch, handed over a phone number for furnished rentals or recommended a sublet?

You've really planned this out, haven't you?

(You'll say your heart is broken, but it won't be true. But that will be the acceptable thing to say. That you are broken-hearted about the whole thing. If you were a poet, like Charlie, you would write a poem about how very sad you are. People will want to know you're in pain, not that you finally feel a happiness that he managed to steal from you for years. All you will really feel is relief. Not happiness, but relief.)

And while you were in that empty room, trying to find a single bowl and a single mug, did you actually think Charlie was going to leave his wife?

Did you actually believe that he would leave the warmth and affection of the mediocre?

Of dinner on the table at seven and sex at ten?

Did you actually think that winning that war for *Ulysses* would mean that you were free?

That you would be happy?

Nothing more than a sigh of relief.

CHAPTER FIFTY

"Noah." Ronnie stared down at the child she'd never met, the one she'd heard Charlie talk about occasionally. The child Charlie had avoided talking about. "Noah." It was as if she was naming him to make him real.

"Noah," he repeated at her, rocking back and forth gently, his hand contorting and tapping an imaginary object in the air. "Noah, Noah, Noah, Noah. Pretty."

The child pointed again. "Pretty."

And in that moment at Charlie's door Ronnie realized she had made a monumental mistake. She heard Charlie call out for Noah from within the house and heard him make his way toward the front door. When he locked eyes with Ronnie the panic was palpable. The anxiety she had managed to assuage returned in a suffocating wave.

Wordless, Charlie stared at her angrily, an astonished fury filling his face.

"Who is it, Charles?" Tamara called from inside the house.

Ronnie looked down at Noah one last time and, soaking wet and smiling at him, began to speak. "I'm sorry, sir. I think I have the wrong house."

"Yes, I'm quite sure you do," Charlie replied. He pulled a squirming, protesting Noah back into the house and shut the door.

CHAPTER FIFTY-ONE

The afternoon the final test results were due back from the hospital, Ronnie went for a walk through the university campus. She was told on the phone to expect them in the late afternoon, and if necessary they would schedule the surgery immediately. The idea of spending that day at home, staring at the phone and the television and the phone and the wall was intolerable.

Ronnie put on her iPod and headed toward the Annex on her bike. She decided to leave her bike helmet behind, imagining the likelihood of a tragic bike accident and news of a hysterectomy on the same afternoon was slim.

By going to the university, Ronnie's aim was not really to be near Charlie, but rather to be in his world, a world that for a short time, less than a year ago, when they first met, was free of disease, a complete escape from the concerned looks and plans and procedures. Charlie was one of those people who constantly worried, yet nothing would ever go wrong for him. For some reason he was protected from harm, one of those blessed people that beauty somehow followed, that happiness hounded, and yet he never saw it. His wife, his child, his Annex home with its yard strewn with toys. He was protected from disaster because it failed to follow him, and yet here was Ronnie, on a slow walk through his world, waiting for disaster to be announced.

Ronnie hadn't seen or spoken to Charlie since she came to his front door that evening. He'd left a handful of messages on her voicemail, the first enraged and the last apologetic, but Ronnie had decided not to respond. The look of terror on his face when he came down that hallway had stuck with her. She wanted him to be relieved that they were finally free from their lies, but instead he was terrified, his hand on the door and on Noah in frantic, protective panic.

"Daddy, pretty," Noah had said, pointing at Ronnie with fervour.

It occurred to her that she had never really expected Charlie would leave his wife. From the beginning it was apparent that Charlie was the kind of person who desperately needed to feel safe, and hotel rooms and clandestine steaks and cigarettes didn't qualify. He was an anxious man, and anxious men couldn't leave the realm of the familiar. They would pretend and talk and dream, but at the end of it all the face of failure was too much to bear.

Ronnie headed into a dive bar near campus and sat down on a stool to order whisky, neat. It was just after Labour Day and school had begun again. There were smiling, laughing girls everywhere, a disproportionate number really, too early in the afternoon for them to be drunk but late enough for them to be jovial. It was too soon for them to have term papers due and it was still warm enough for them to be dressed in summer clothes, their skin golden-brown and pink with the sun, surrounded by open books they were strategically ignoring. A small group of girls in horn-rimmed glasses and shaggy haircuts were knitting together in focused, blissful silence, while bleached blonde girls in painted-on U of T T-shirts gossiped about last night's conquests. Everyone seemed to be drinking cheap domestic beer.

The girls collectively made Ronnie feel so old. It was true that Charlie had an ability to make Ronnie feel suddenly young, but the reality was in the bar.

Beautiful young things did not border on the wrong side of thirty-five, nor did they wait to find out if they needed hysterectomies while drinking whisky neat.

Her cellphone rang.

CHAPTER FIFTY-TWO

Ronnie wasn't returning his messages.

Charlie no longer knew whose fault that was.

Charlie had been in breakups before. It had been decades ago, but he remembered how they worked.

His male writer friends would get together and discuss their innumerable conquests and breakups over pints and cigars, talking about disposed women with mocking laughter. Their bravado generally appalled him, small men destroying with words the women who had destroyed them, but it was all so transparent; they were wounded like teenagers, aging like relics.

Breakups meant that a woman you used to think you knew would come to your house in the middle of the night, while you were sleeping, and steal all of your patio furniture from your backyard.

Breakups meant that the charred remains of your belongings would be stuffed in a black plastic garbage bag and left on the front porch to greet you when you got home from work.

Breakups meant an excruciating conversation in the produce section of the supermarket. It meant long, awkward waits for a teller at the bank while the object of your burning affection was three people in front of you, and the whole time you were standing there you repeatedly prayed she wouldn't turn around and see you.

It meant dividing bank accounts, vinyl collections, and friends. It meant vitriol. It meant the vilest elements of the human condition condensed into a progression of failing to freedom.

Charlie didn't want that to happen with Tamara, and he certainly didn't want that to happen with Ronnie. Instead he preferred to suspend himself in stasis, inaction, paralysis—retreating to the quiet of his at-home office, locking the door behind him, and staying there deep into the night. Only Amanda would ever come to the door, usually before she left for the night, her exceedingly cheerful voice offering a cup of cocoa or a plate of warmed leftovers when her worry prompted her to do so. He would pour another whisky and call through the door that he was fine and she should go.

Ronnie wasn't speaking to him, but they hadn't yet broken up. His wife could sense that something was wrong, but didn't know anything for sure. It was a period of pause, and Charlie walked around numbly, helplessly, pouring the only energy he had into a novel of exceeding optimism, a manuscript that sketched out a nauseatingly happy ending that Charlie knew would never come to be.

He would stay in his office chair until late became early, typing search terms like "divorce," "infidelity," "polyamory," and "cervical cancer" into his browser. Communities of the betrayed popped up, with their sad, self-pitying digital consolations. Other searches revealed legal jargon, lavish tales of fulfilled lifestyles, and a mysterious world of impromptu vaginal bleeding. He read the numerous ways in which Ronnie could die, the endless statistics on how promising her chance was to live. How the surgery might save her. He wanted to call her and tell her to eat more kale, take vitamin C, and stop smoking after they had sex.

He longed to tell his wife he needed to take care of Ronnie, that it didn't matter to him that taking care of someone's future wife, someone other than his own wife, was wrong.

There were moments of clarity, usually caused by films or music or books, moments when he knew that he loved Ronnie, and that nothing should ever matter more than that love. But life wasn't a song or a film or a movie. Life was Tamara and Noah and the very expensive proposition of a divorce and his inability to support himself and the ongoing disappointment that Charlie had become. Life was selling the house and splitting their things and splitting their friends. Life was the infidelity that would be the cause of him never seeing Noah again.

He knew what people would say when they found out. They would claim Charlie was nothing more that the self-indulgent poet with a pretty little hairdresser on the side. The more sympathetic would believe that she was fine for a dalliance but certainly not good enough to marry, and that he should have learned to keep his secrets better. There was a part of Charlie that now believed this to be true.

So in the office, deep into the night, Charlie sat in stasis. Waiting for a message that never came.

Because love did not conquer all. Love just made it easier for all to conquer you.

With Ronnie's silence Charlie realized fully that he had gotten lazy. Staring into the evidence of his affair, reading and re-reading her messages over and over in the silence, he saw that he had collected a monolith of damning details that were nothing more than a password away. Where once he had purged his cellphone messages and emails daily and disposed of hotel and dinner receipts at the office, he'd become less concerned about getting caught and left markers of his infidelity in pants and coat pockets. This likely was a function of his recent willingness to get caught, the notion that perhaps things would be easier if he was simply ejected from his life rather than summoning the strength to leave it.

And while his overall concern over being discovered by these paper reminders decreased, his ability to lie had improved. Each suspect artifact became easier and easier to explain away. He had booked a hotel in the afternoon to find some space to write. He had gone to dinner with a promising young writer to win favour with the faculty for future gigs. He'd bought flowers for a beleaguered colleague whose cat had just succumbed to feline leukemia. The lies got better and more complicated. They just came out of his mouth like fluid fiction, one after another, sometimes about things that weren't even necessary to lie about. It became a game, and as time progressed he was more than sure he would never be caught.

Charlie was raised to feel like philanderers always got busted at some point, that discovery was inevitable, but as months progressed and he shamelessly touched the small of Ronnie's back in public, shamelessly kissed her fingertips over dinner, had her in innumerable hotel rooms and signed for their room service naked, he began to imagine that discovery was not only impossible, but that no one truly cared enough about his tiny little life to out him for indiscretion.

The truth was that betrayal was only ever discovered when those involved wanted it to be revealed. People only tell lies that other people want to live in. In fact, he concluded, liars were generous because they created a comfortable space in which the deluded happily chose to live.

"Honey, is there something wrong? You seem distant," Tamara asked one night, her voice a mixture of concern and suspicion, as they sat in from of the television.

"It's nothing. I'm just struggling with the book," Charlie lied.

"Do I tell you enough that I'm proud of you?"

Tamara was deluded. Comfortable and deluded, and he would construct a world of untruths around her to keep her safe. He would lie until she decided it was no longer comfortable for her to rely on that safety.

CHAPTER FIFTY-THREE

Tamara came into the salon on a Wednesday afternoon. Ronnie had no idea who she was, nothing more than a new client as she sat down in Ronnie's chair and asked for "not too much off."

It was the start of the Christmas shopping season, which made the streets pedestrian heavy and the salon endlessly busy. Ronnie was distracted and flustered and didn't give the woman a second thought as she stared intensely at her in the mirror.

Ronnie had never seen pictures of Tamara, even though she had scoured the Internet for an image to compare herself to. She had even asked Charlie for a photo and he had refused.

"So what are we doing today?" Ronnie asked, her stock haircut question.

"We're going to talk about why you're fucking my husband," was Tamara's reply.

Sarah had finally called Tamara, one evening when she had had one Chardonnay too many, when she was bored, seated at her kitchen table in her lonely one-bedroom apartment with her cat named Mittens. She knew Charlie was out, doing a reading at the library, and the truth was she was tired of him having two when she couldn't even have one.

The declaration was direct and made with no attempt to soften the blow. Sarah was the kind of person who felt great joy in exposing people's moral failings, and she was righteous about the delivery. She of course was met with denial, anger, shock, and then misery.

Noah clung to Tamara's waist and screamed nonsensical sentences up at her as the tears came, but Sarah didn't relent.

"I've even *heard* them. Do you understand what I mean? *I've heard them.*"

"Yes, Sarah. Thank you. I understand."

Sarah cared little for how Tamara might feel about this piece of information, cared little about the fact that Tamara's stomach dropped and she was consumed by a weakness that forced her to hang onto the doorframe next to the phone. She felt like she may vomit, but Sarah just kept talking, outlining her personal opinions on the sin of infidelity.

"Yes, Sarah, I understand. I understand. Thank you for calling," Tamara said numbly, hanging up the phone while Sarah was mid-sentence.

She proceeded to wander around their home, attempting to find any evidence to back up Sarah's claims. Sarah had provided only a name.

Veronica.

Ronnie.

Every pocket was picked through, every closet, and drawer emptied in a frantic tour around their home. After rummaging through Charlie's desk she found *Veronica Kline*'s business card.

Where was Charlie?
He said he was in a meeting.
He said he was running errands.
He said he was working with a student.
He said he was on a roll with the new novel.
He said. He said. He said.

A fucking hairdresser.

Noah, underfoot, knew something was wrong. He began shrieking, inconsolable, pounding his fists on his thighs. Tamara could do nothing, only stare at the card, reading it over and over again as if to confirm it was real.

Veronica Kline. A simple girl. A hairdresser. Subject of a new novel. The novel he hadn't let her read.

He had always let her read. She was his first reader. His fiercest critic. Why hadn't she seen a single page of this one?

She called the following morning to make an appointment for a cut and colour.

Ronnie stood frozen, taking in the accusation with disbelief, despite the fact that she had prepared endlessly for this moment. That it was inevitable.

"I'm sorry?" she asked, as if it had escaped her that she was indeed having an affair. Or had been having an affair. She wasn't really sure at this point.

"Let me be as clear as possible. You're going to cut my hair and colour my hair and tell me all about your relationship with my husband. I'll pay you and tip you and then I'll go home and kick him out."

Amazingly, Ronnie began combing out Tamara's hair. Before she replied she took the time to thoroughly survey the woman she had been so jealous of for so many months. Shaking slightly, her cheeks flushed, Ronnie parted Tamara's damp hair down the centre and surveyed the grey. She took indirect glances at the crinkled folds around her eyes, the thickness around her waistline, the fading of the fabric of her clothes.

A mother. Noah's mother. A mother she could never be.

Then she looked at her longingly in the mirror and tried to

understand why this woman, as unremarkable as she seemed, had the capacity to make Charlie stay for so long. Why this woman had existed as a perccived barrier to her happiness.

Ronnie knew she suddenly had the power to tell her everything, to have Tamara eject him into a life that could only lead to her. To unburden herself of all of it and move on if she wanted to. This thought terrified her, the power she suddenly wielded.

"I'm sorry. I don't know what you're talking about."

"Please don't be patronizing. You know exactly what I'm talking about. Tell me about your relationship with my husband."

Ronnie knew there was little point in lying. It was over.

"I went to his office. I tried to sleep with him," she said slowly, carefully combing, not making eye contact.

Tamara, however, stared as Ronnie began to strategically part her hair. She noticed that Ronnie was shaking slightly as she reached for her scissors out of her belt.

"Don't worry. While I think it's disgusting that you'd try to fuck a married man, that you'd fuck a married man, I'm not really all that interested in being angry at you. You have no responsibility toward my family. What the fuck would you care?"

"I do care."

Tamara laughed loudly at this idea. "Please. Spare me. And do your job. I'm paying you."

Despite the rudeness of Tamara's direction, Ronnie knew she would be fine if only she could get to the cutting. She had to get to the cutting. The cutting always made her feel better. It was the ability to control something so minor, yet something that people vainly valued so much.

But this time she was confused by who had control.

Tamara continued when it was evident Ronnie had no plans to

reply. "Whether or not you care is completely irrelevant to me. But I am curious; what would possess you to go and try to fuck someone's husband? Why would you think that was a good idea? I'm really interested to know, given that I've always wondered what kind of woman would do such a thing."

Tamara seemed oddly composed. It was this fact that most unnerved Ronnie, and she finally started cutting to steady herself.

"I thought I loved him," she finally said after a dozen excruciating snips.

"Did you, now?"

"But he told me he loved you. And Noah. And he couldn't."

Tamara flinched at the sound of her son's name, but then managed to regain her composure. "I don't believe you. While it's sweet that you'd try to cover for him, I don't believe you."

"I don't care if you don't believe me. That's what happened."

The lies had always come so easily.

"You know it doesn't actually matter what you say at this point because no matter what he's packing his bags tonight. He doesn't know it yet but he is. So you might as well unburden yourself."

"There's nothing to unburden."

"Oh dear god, please. Don't waste my fucking time. You owe me at least that. If you owe me anything you owe me that."

"I wanted him. He wanted you. That's it."

"Maybe I should get my hair cut and coloured just like yours," Tamara said.

It was then she started crying, her face strained from the effort to keep it in.

"Maybe I should be twenty years younger. Just like you. What are you, twenty-three? Twenty-four?"

"I'm thirty-five," Ronnie responded weakly.

"Oh god, he can't even cheat on me with someone too young for him. For fuck's sake."

Ronnie replaced the scissors on the ledge next to the mirror. For a moment she considered putting her hands on Tamara's shoulders but resisted.

"Are you married?"

"Engaged."

"Does your fiancé know you tried to fuck my husband? Excuse me. That you fucked my husband? That you fucked my husband over and over and over again?"

Tamara's volume had increased and she was attracting Lisa's attention, who was doing a cut a few chairs over. Lisa shot Ronnie an "are you okay" look in the mirror.

Ronnie nodded feebly in Lisa's direction.

"No, he doesn't. Know. That I tried to."

Lisa gave the look that acknowledged she knew what was going on. She took a step forward, hesitated, and then took a step back.

"Yeah, I didn't think so. You're a coward just like my husband. Why aren't you cutting?"

"I'm sorry but I think you should go," she said, putting her hands down firmly at her sides.

"Did you fuck my husband, Veronica?"

"I can get someone else here to cut your hair if you like. Lisa would be happy to help you."

Lisa looked up again at the sound of her own name.

"Did you fuck my husband, Veronica?" Louder this time.

"Please—"

"Did you fuck my husband, Veronica?"

Finally Lisa interjected. "Listen, lady. I think my friend here asked you to leave."

"I don't think this concerns you, unless you're having an affair with my husband as well. Which could totally be possible," Tamara responded, still articulate enough that it seemed impossible. Lisa, with all her bravado, went suddenly pale, unable to properly respond.

Suddenly Ronnie exploded. "Yes, yes. Yes, I fucked your husband. Please just go."

The other patrons turned to stare, without empathy, only with disdain.

"Thank you. You should offer your fiancé the same courtesy you just offered me." With her hair damp and partially cut, Tamara picked up her coat and bag and went home to kick Charlie out.

(CHAPTER FIFTY-FOUR)   *185*

A toothpaste-blue open-backed gown and a pasty white shower cap for her hair. Aaron in a paper face mask, clutching her limp hand apologetically.

She had consoled him, told him it would be okay, she would be okay, but he had cried regardless, looking haggard under the unforgiving fluorescents.

While he waited he ate from the vending machine and masochistically wandered through maternity.

"Veronica. I'm going to need you to count backward from one hundred for me, okay?" the pretty blonde nurse with the IV said sweetly as the others prepared below.

One hundred, ninety-nine, ninety-eight, ninety-seven . . .
Everything was.
Ninety-six, ninety-five, ninety-four, ninety-three . . .
And then it wasn't.
Ninety-two, ninety-one, ninety . . .
It was. Then it wasn't.

"Veronica?"

It was. And then it was gone.

(CHAPTER FIFTY-FIVE)

People who commit infidelity all seem to end up in the same shitty
hotel room. There's no room service and the concierge charges you
a "glass fee" when you bring your own wine in from the Wine Rack
on Wellesley. You have to sign a form promising you're not going
to smoke, and when you've had enough of that bottle of wine, you
contemplate paying the $300 cleaning fee just to take a few hauls off
a Marlboro. You remember how you used to tell her not to smoke,
but now you no longer care, because it feels like she no longer cares
about you. You no longer care about yourself.

   The shitty hotel is always in a bad neighbourhood and it is always grossly overpriced. It is definitely across the street from a park
where people deal drugs and fuck for money.

   The shitty hotel room is not like the grossly overpriced beautiful hotel rooms you made love to her in. There is no room service menu here and certainly no adjacent spa. No terry cloth bathrobes that slip from her shoulder as she raises her glass of champagne or sucks on a strawberry.

Instead there are crack whores on the street outside and screaming white trash children in the fluorescent-lit "dining lounge." There is a paper bag of bad takeout on the chipped coffee table. You watch the drug deals from the window. You have twenty-two channels and there is no pay-per-view. There is certainly no her. She is "giving you some time and space to think about things" because she knows that your wife has figured things out. The fact that your wife has figured things out has rendered you immediately unattractive.

She knows that really you're figuring out a way to get back to your wife. You're ashamed of this, but it's the truth. You wanted them both the way you wanted them, and you hate yourself for this.

And your wife does not call you, nor does she care where you have gone. There are no emails, no text messages, no smoke signals. She came home and gave you twenty minutes to pack a meagre bag without any indication of when she will let you come back, if at all. She didn't speak. She just hovered over you while you packed, made sure you didn't take anything that wasn't rightfully yours.

So you chose the things you took with you carefully. Just enough to last if she doesn't ever let you come back, but just too little to ensure that you'll have a reason to return.

"I need to pick up my electric razor, Tamara."

She will ask you to come to the house, the house you once shared, when she's at work, when Noah's at the playground with Amanda, when it is completely empty. She will not want to know that you came and she will not want to know that you looked through old photos and touched Noah's toys and laid down in the bed the two of you slept in together and breathed in the scent of what was once your bodies entwined. The smell faint, because it rarely happened, if ever. But now that you're living in a shitty hotel room in a bad neighbourhood, you remember it fondly. It wasn't thrilling or remotely sexual or even exciting, but it was safe and warm and real, so much more so than this cold hotel room and this chipped wineglass and this moment where you wonder why you bothered in the first place.

(CHAPTER FIFTY-SIX)

"So you're gonna write a whole book about me, eh?" Tamara had said that first night, while draining her third pint.

"For such a little thing, you certainly can drink."

"There's a lot of things I can do. Likely better than you, anointed one."

"You need to stop calling me that."

"Does success make you blush, Mr. Stern?"

"Certainly more than my compliments make you blush."

"Call me cynical, but I don't trust your lot."

"Men or poets?"

Tamara laughed. "Probably both, actually. Never trust a man who has a way with words."

"Would you prefer me a grunting fool?"

"I think there's a dirty joke in there somewhere."

"You know, Tamara, I think that you may bring out a masterpiece in me," Charlie said, drunkenly yet with complete sincerity.

"But honey, you just met me." Tamara stood up, removing her soft grey cardigan from the back of her chair and attempting to thread her arms into it. She stumbled a bit, grasping his shoulder to steady herself. "Thanks for the drinks by the way."

Charlie realized it was her intention to leave and downed his own pint a little too quickly. His companions had all gone home one by one, each of them giving him that knowing glance of good luck in bringing Tamara back to his place for the evening. He had his mind set on it now and was groping for a reason for her to come with him.

"Hey, Tamara. Do you want to come back to my place and I can read you some more of my poems? There's some new things I've been working on that I think you might like—"

Tamara burst into a fit of laughter. "Oh god. You are joking, right?"

"Well, I just thought, given your new interest in poetry you might want to hear a few more."

Charlie was embarrassed, but Tamara bent down slowly and touched the side of his face with her soft hand.

"Listen. I'll come home with you, Charlie. And I don't need the promise of poetry to do it."

(CHAPTER FIFTY-SEVEN)

"I want custody of Noah. Entirely."

Charlie and Tamara were seated across the dining room table

from each other. So many dinners, so many evenings where they loved or hated or tolerated each other across the same table flashed in Charlie's mind.

"You cut your hair. It looks good," he said, trying to change the subject, trying to soften the mood.

She self-consciously put a hand to her head, her hair now a full five inches shorter after her own stylist corrected the half-haircut Veronica had given. Charlie took the haircut as a bad sign, a purging of him from her life, when really he should have recognized it as a much worse sign. He hadn't yet been informed that Tamara and Ronnie had together decided his fate.

Charlie had a tumbler of whisky and Tamara a glass of milk. Noah was snug in bed, put there by a beleaguered Amanda, who knew something was afoot but hadn't been officially told. Charlie himself looked dishevelled . . . tired, unshaven, his clothes wrinkled. He smelled bad, a function of his limited access to laundry. She had invited him to the house via email, refusing to speak to him on the phone for countless days, saying they needed to discuss things. Charlie had assumed it would be a moment where he could plead his case to return, but it was evident immediately that the meeting was about dividing assets.

"Tamara, I want to come home."

"I don't give a fuck what you want."

"Please. We can talk about this."

"There's nothing to talk about. I want custody of Noah. I'll let you know when you can visit him."

"I have no plans to fight you," he said meekly.

"I want the house. All of it. You can take your records and your books."

"Tamara. I—I can't afford the hotel anymore."

"That's your reasoning for coming home? Because you need me to financially support you?"

"No. I just . . . I can't do it anymore. I need to see you. Every day."

"You just said you wouldn't fight me."

"Please . . ."

"I spent my whole life taking care of you. Being the dutiful wife. I'm done."

"I can't do this. I can't do this without you," Charlie said, on the verge of weeping.

"What is this about? Did Veronica leave you? Did I scare her off?"

"What do you mean? Scare her off?"

"Charlie, don't make this harder than it needs to be."

"What do you mean, Tamara?"

The horror of what this implied sunk in, and Charlie suddenly realized why he hadn't heard from Veronica. He decided not to press, despite the fact that the idea of his wife meeting his lover was enough to bring on the panic attack that was creeping up his spine.

"I just want to see you," he said, changing direction.

"Well you're seeing me now and I'm telling you . . . I don't expect any support from you, not that you could provide it anyway. In exchange I want sole custody of Noah. And I want the house. I don't care where you live. Go live with Veronica for all I care."

"She's not returning my calls," Charlie said. As soon as he did so he realized the statement was unwise.

"I knew it."

"But I wouldn't want to see her anyway," Charlie said, backpedalling.

"Whatever. I couldn't care less. Noah. The house. I'm done supporting you. You can do whatever you like."

"Tamara. Please. Listen."

"It's over. Please, if you have anything good left inside you, just let me move on."

He wondered, *Is there anything good left?*

Tamara began to cry, and as Charlie raised the tumbler to his mouth for a final burning gulp, he caught a glimpse of the inside of his wrist.

A tiny tattooed anchor, grounding him to nothing.

(CHAPTER FIFTY-EIGHT)

Tamara is good. Aaron is good. Ronnie is bad. Charlie is bad.

Noah is good. Noah is better than all of this.

If you want to make a real go of life, to become something accepted and acceptable, and you are bad, it's best to go out and find yourself someone good and fake it. Pretend you are good enough for them and just go with it. Pretending is your only way out. Let their perfection blot out the ugly parts of yourself, hide in their beauty so no one notices how truly flawed you are.

It can be excruciating, sitting through dinners with in-laws and friends (*good* friends) where you pretend to be good and good enough. It will be hard to listen to people tell you how lucky you are to have found someone so good. (Note how they never say "good *for you*" or that the other person is lucky to have found you. No. You were someone who was destined to end up nowhere and instead was rescued by one of *the good*. You are blessed. You are a broken thing that has been salvaged. Remember that.)

Feel blessed.

Sure, you may have an initial feeling of being a fraud. Feeling so alien. And it'll fuck you right up. But that feeling will go away eventually. You'll numb yourself to it in time. In some ways you'll numb yourself to everything. You'll be numb to all the things you wanted before, the adventure you thought you'd carve from life, all the desires for something more than this mundane life of being "good."

You'll be loved and accepted and an "acceptable member of society." There will be a quiet calm. You'll go to bed early and wake up early and pay your bills on time and have good, normal, acceptable sex in a good, normal, acceptable bed an acceptable number of times a week. And you'll actually start to believe you're happy. The mediocre will grow on you. The limp way you hold hands in the supermarket. The way you get a light kiss in the condiments aisle for saying something slightly witty. You'll be told you're cute and smart and you'll finally feel worth loving.

You might even begin to forget you're bad. You might even begin to think that it was all a phase, that you're finally ready to be good.

That everything will work out okay in the end.

But the key to maintaining this kind of happiness is to never again get too close to someone who is bad like you were. Even if they're reformed bad, the two of you together will just sink down into your former cesspool, like alcoholics relapsing together is a fuzzy haze of feel-good despair. You'll remember the familiar feelings. You'll remember the freedom of four a.m. whisky shots. You'll remember the way lies tasted sweeter than the truth, and inevitably you'll end up in a hotel room at one in the afternoon with your clothes strewn around the room. You'll end up grasping at something and being completely unsure what it us, you'll just scratch and dig at it until there's nothing left. And despite the destruction, the discomfort, you'll know it's so much better than your current, "good" life. Your credit card will be maxed out and the sheets will be fine and filthy and the taste of him on your mouth sweet. And you will long for him in ways you never even imagined possible. You will yearn and ache and cry drunk in bathroom stalls. You'll break down inappropriately in grocery stores. You'll run away in the middle of the night. You'll never want to come back. You'll crave him in ways you never thought possible to crave another human being. You'll see him and be torn in two.

And he is bad. He is bad for you. He is everything you knew it was best to stay away from. You watch him shake and twitch with anxiety over the smallest, most insignificant moments. You don't know how to help him and you're not sure you want to. He exhausts you. You are exhausted. You want him to love you but you find yourself not caring if he does. You feel yourself creeping from good to bad. You feel the weight of your double life. You feel it all. You feel everything in a way you never did before. And you hate him for it. And you love him for it. You remember the days when you were numb to everything. Where nothing could hurt you. And then all of a sudden he is hurting you. He is hurting you with his distance and he is hurting you with his closeness and he is destroying you by merely being alive.

And he is worth it. And he is not worth it. And you are sorry. And you are not sorry. And you feel guilty. And you don't feel guilty. And it doesn't matter. And it doesn't matter. And it doesn't matter.

It will never matter.

Because you are so small and insignificant and no one will remember and no one will forget.

Because no one really cares that you made love to Charlie in a bed at the Westin Harbour Castle. Or the Garden Hilton. Or the Marriott. Or on his desk in his office. Or in a bathroom stall at Robarts.

And you realize the promise to be good gets you nowhere. Being good gets you unhappy and it gets you lonely and it gets you a life you never wanted in the first place. It gets you loveless. And empty. And numb.

And it doesn't get you Charlie.

Charlie laments the way the waitress fails to bring the creamer, the way his meeting got cancelled, the way the cab driver gets lost on a Sunday afternoon when you both have nowhere to be. Charlie disappears for days, weeks at a time. Charlie doesn't reply, and when you are not available Charlie panics. You loathe the way he looks away from you, fear the way he ignores you when he's with his family, with Noah, but as soon as he is with you, as soon as you wrap your limbs around his and hold on tight, the hate is gone.

Because he is forgiven. Because you are forgiven. This is forgiveness, being this close to love, however far away it seems. This is the kind of forgiveness for being human you cannot get from mediocre handholding in supermarkets. This is the kind of love you were always so sure existed when you were a child. This is the kind of real your mother claimed could never be true. This is better than taking what you are given, which is what you were always instructed to do.

This, with all the lies that keep it together, is more truth than you have ever known.

(CHAPTER FIFTY-NINE)

"Charlie, we have to end this. For good. You need to stop calling me."

He had known it was coming. That it had in fact already come, but that he needed to hear her to say it.

"It's not healthy for either of us, and I need to take some time to take care of myself right now."

"Why, Ronnie? Why do you need to take care of yourself right now?"

It had been weeks and weeks and he had been sending message after message to Ronnie with no response. While he was making real efforts to repair things with Tamara from his hotel room across town, he obsessively checked his email for a sign from Ronnie.

"Tell me you're okay, Ronnie. I worry about you. I miss you so much. Please. I just want to see you."

"Charlie, you know I can't do that. Not after what happened. Now that your wife knows. Now that you've decided. Now that you've chosen."

He wanted to know if she was crying. It would mean something if she was crying.

"I just need some time, Ronnie. Some time to fix things. I told you that. I need you to be patient."

"Too many things have happened, Charlie. Things are different now."

In his messages he had explained at length how he was sorry, how important it was to try to mend a marriage, that there were so many more people to consider than merely himself. That people were counting on him to be a good husband and father and he couldn't let them down.

Ronnie was pretty sure that this was all a lie, that the reason he was attempting to repair his marriage was because he was terrified of losing the comforts he had grown accustomed to, financial and otherwise. That he was terrified of what other people would think of him. Charlie was gifted at the cultivation of shame; the idea that colleagues, friends, and family would see him as the man whose wife left him and took their child with her was more devastating than the loss of Ronnie in his life.

"What has happened, Ronnie? Tell me what has happened."

All the freedom he needed to see Ronnie was finally his, in his hotel room where he was never expected to go home, and she was nowhere to be found. The colliding of his life with hers, how real it had all become at his front door and at her place of work, had proven too much for her to handle.

"Answer me, Ronnie. *What* has happened?"

"Nothing. It just isn't right anymore. It isn't fun anymore," she said.

Fun? he thought. *What a strange word to use.*

"Will it do any good if I ask you to come back to me?" Charlie asked, defeated.

"No, Charlie. It's too late for that now."

Ronnie knew that love couldn't conquer all. It certainly could conquer most, but it could never erase the reality that Charlie would need to be housed and fed when he was writing poetry. Ronnie's insecurities that she was somehow lesser than Charlie because she didn't have a "calling," as she put it, were entirely false. Charlie's calling had made him weak and needy. It made him dependent on Tamara and the stability she constantly provided.

"Charlie, we have to end this. For good. I don't think you should email or call me anymore."

"Please don't. Please don't go. Please just see me one more time. Just one more."

"It's no use. There's no point."

"I want to kiss you one more time. Touch you one more time."

"Don't embarrass yourself, Charlie."

"There's got to be something worth saving. Anything?"

While it seemed Ronnie had achieved what she had been looking for . . . Charlie without wife . . . she knew the split only increased his longing for his family. Ronnie was wary of consoling him while he lamented the loss. While Charlie spoke mostly of missing Noah, Ronnie knew it was more than that.

When an affair ends, it is difficult to pinpoint why and how it started in the first place.

A witty joke, a shared cookie, and a shot glass in a pocket?

The brashness of writing an unsolicited letter?

A flask of peach schnapps?

A lemon-yellow dress and a fuck in the afternoon?

Ronnie knew Charlie wanted his wife, his life, and while Charlie sobbed Tamara's name and drank himself to sleep in that terrible hotel room on Jarvis, Ronnie spent time convincing herself that she would find away to dissolve the affair.

She was convinced.

"There's nothing real to hold on to here. There never was."

(CHAPTER SIXTY)

Charlie stumbled around U of T campus in the early spring rain a wounded, lost man, a bottle of whisky concealed in his jacket. He knew that Tamara had Noah and Ronnie had Aaron and that he only had a whisky bottle and a manuscript about a girl he could no longer fuck. The idea of finishing the novel was terrifying; excessive amounts of time spent in a world he'd created to celebrate Ronnie.

A waste.

He would attempt to work in the library, in a café, at the bar, anywhere but the sad, dark hotel room that had become his home, an award-winning author without a real place to write. The time he spent pretending to work was bearable, but when he returned to his room on Jarvis Street he found he would fall into a pit of longing that only drinking could float him out of.

He would pick up the phone to call Ronnie and then hang up before all the numbers were dialled.

He would pick up the phone to call Tamara and then hang up before the numbers were dialled.

He would fanaticize about confronting Aaron, letting him know that he loved Ronnie more than he ever could.

He rehearsed the scenes in his head over and over, composing the words he would say to each of them to repair the situation to his liking, imagining he had the courage for each confrontation.

But he knew that simply wasn't true.

"We have to end this, not that there's much to end anymore," Ronnie would say.

"You're an amazing woman, Veronica," he would say.

(CHAPTER SIXTY-ONE)

Ronnie came in from the back porch just as Aaron returned to the apartment from running errands. She clutched a red lipstick–smeared wineglass and inhaled deeply as she heard his key in the lock. Ramona scrambled toward the front door to greet him, her claws echoing against the hardwood floor as she slid to a stop and jumped to his chest.

"Ronnie? I'm home," he called from the front hall.

She said nothing, placing her wineglass gently on the counter and waiting.

"Have you been smoking?" Aaron asked the moment he saw her, a look of disdain clearly on his face as he put down his gym bag and unpacked a small bag of groceries onto their kitchen counter.

"Why yes, Aaron. I have been smoking."

"Why would you do that when . . ."

"We're going to have a baby? Have a baby? Have a fucking baby? Is that what you were going to say?" Ronnie's volume was steadily increasing. "You got so used to saying it, now you've forgotten that we can't have a baby?"

"I was going to say while you're still healing, actually."

"I'm fine. I'm healed," she said, tipping back her glass of wine dramatically.

"And we can still have a baby, you know. I don't understand why you have to be so dramatic. I know you're upset about the surgery, that we can't have our own, but lots of . . ."

"Oh, just shut up. We've been trying to have a baby for three years. I'm tired. Let me fucking be dramatic. Let me fucking smoke."

"Jesus. What is wrong with you? Are you drunk?"

"I can't have a fucking baby, Aaron. There will never be a baby. They've sliced me open. Cut me in half to take out my ability to have a baby."

"Don't say that. Stop saying that. It's gruesome."

"Why not? Because it's true? Because there's all sorts of things that are true that we never talk about? That we've never talked about? And you're fucking worried about me smoking?"

"What things we never talk about?"

"Everything, Aaron. Absolutely everything. We haven't been talking for years and you know it."

"You're fucking drunk."

"And you're in complete denial."

This was the moment.

She knew it before it happened.

This was the moment that would send a new set of circumstances into motion. The clarity of it was striking. Whatever Ronnie said from this point on would set them on a trajectory that would never be undone.

"What the fuck is wrong with you?"

What was wrong with Ronnie was that she had forgotten herself. While she smoked half a pack of cigarettes and drank half a bottle of Merlot on their back deck this became increasingly clear. She knew she loved Charlie with the kind of love that reaffirms life, wanted Charlie even now, but while submerged in him she became the opposite of what Aaron wanted her to be.

"I think I need to leave, Aaron."

"What, like, go out? Like go to the store? Go to a friend's house? Go on vacation?"

"No, leave. Leave this apartment. Leave the city. Leave the country. Leave you."

"Leave? For fuck's sake, Veronica. We're supposed to get married in a week. What the fuck are you talking about?"

"I need to leave you, Aaron."

"Stop it."

"I think we should cancel the wedding."

Aaron remained silent for a moment. His fingers curled into fists and his face flushed red. Ramona had wandered in and stared up at them from the kitchen floor, sitting eagerly, right paw lifted, intent on getting a dog treat from one of them. She had never been one for real empathy or even awareness, completely oblivious to what was coming.

The trajectory of what was coming.

"I don't believe you. I can't believe you. You're overtired."

"I don't need you to believe me. I just need to go. I don't know who I am anymore."

"You're Ronnie! You're my wife, Ronnie! That's who the fuck you are."

"No, I'm not. And I don't know if I can be next week."

Aaron's face changed dramatically. "Don't you love me?"

Ronnie recognized this part. It was the pleading part where things became awful, where no amount of confidence or certainty can make them not awful. Aaron leaned back on the kitchen counter and then slowly sank to the ground, putting his face in his hands. The dog got up and wandered over to him, sniffing and licking the exposed parts of his face. A guttural noise erupted from within him, a noise she hadn't heard him produce before. It sounded like a tortured animal, the kind of gasping, heaving cry that comes only from the knowledge of real grief.

"Of course I love you, Aaron. I'll always love you. I'll love you forever."

"Ronnie. Please don't."

"But I can't marry you," she said softy, quietly.

"You just have cold feet. That's all. You'll get used to it."

"Aaron, I need you to sleep somewhere else tonight. Just while I get some things together. Okay?"

"This sort of thing happens all the time. My guy friends say this always happens. They warned me about this. You'll get over it. I understand. It'll pass."

"Aaron. I need you to leave."

"Veronica."

"Please leave."

And it was done.

CHAPTER SIXTY-TWO

Aaron slowly packed a small overnight bag while Ronnie watched. She leaned against the doorframe of their bedroom while he folded a shirt and placed it into his backpack. She was adamant about him leaving and her uncertainty about the wedding left him weak enough to agree. While he was reluctant to leave her alone, he believed that if he gave her the space she desired, checked into a hotel for an evening, she would grow to miss him, realize her mistake, and beg for him to come back.

"Call Lisa. Call your mom. Talk to them about how you feel and let them convince you you're making a big mistake. I'm coming back tomorrow morning. And next week we're fucking getting married."

"Aaron, just go."

He had heard about this phenomenon before, women becoming doubtful that a union was the best plan, panicking and sending their to-be-weds away for a brief moment before the walk down the aisle went ahead as scheduled. He could handle this. It was no problem. She just needed a night to get her thoughts in order.

Aaron had catered an event at a hotel on Jarvis a month before, so it was the first place he thought of, called to make a reservation

203

with the phone number he still had in his cellphone, the one he had once used to make food delivery arrangements. They let him know a room was available for one night and that he could check in immediately, so he kissed Ronnie goodbye, only to find she turned her head away from him when he did.

He hailed a cab on Queen and paid the nearly twenty-dollar cab fare to get there.

Lulled into the comfortable belief that she would come round if only he gave her some space, by the time he checked into the hotel, lay out on the bed, and put the news on, he was actually calm and relaxed. To him her reluctance was merely a stage in the process, a thing on the wedding to-do list that had finally been crossed off, and in a few days she would be fine. By the time it got dark he was so deluded he decided to go down to the hotel bar and have a drink to celebrate the milestone.

He asked the bartender for a pint and then surveyed the bar for possible conversation. The only three people there were a couple, likely American tourists with sprawling waistlines and slogan T-shirts on, and an older man scrawling in a notebook at the other end of the bar.

He looked reasonably sane enough.

"What you writing?" Aaron asked.

The man looked up slowly, dazed. His face was haggard, and Aaron immediately noticed he was unshaven and his clothes were rumpled. Perhaps the assumption of sanity had come too quickly. For a moment he regretted asking the question and wondered why he had.

"Excuse me?" the man asked with slight disdain.

"Sorry, never mind. It's really none of my business," Aaron said, returning to his pint.

The man composed himself and instead offered a meek smile.

"Oh, I'm sorry. No, it's fine. It's nothing. Just notes for something I'm working on."

"You a business guy?"

"No, I'm a writer."

"Oh wow, like books?"

"Poems, novels."

"Have I heard of you?"

"I doubt it."

"So what's this book about?" Aaron said, gesturing toward the notebook.

"A girl," he said, concealing the fact that the "what's it about" question was his least favourite hazard of being of writer.

Aaron laughed. "Yeah, this beer's about a girl." He raised his glass in the man's direction.

The man's face softened a bit, and he laughed, as if he recognized a sympathetic ear. He raised his glass in solidarity.

Aaron's pint was close to empty so he motioned the bartender over for another. "Can I get you something? On me?"

There was hesitation. "Sure. Whisky. On the rocks."

The bartender brought another round as the men began chatting. Aaron moved down a few stools and thrust his hand out and introduced himself. "Aaron."

"Charlie."

"Nice to meet you, Charlie."

"So what did your girl do to you?"

"We're supposed to get married next week and she's got some cold feet. That's all. I'm sure it's nothing. I'm just giving her space."

"I'm sure. You know how women can be," Charlie said, realizing how ridiculous his agreement sounded.

"Yeah. I'm sure she'll be calling me any minute, begging me to come back."

Charlie noticed the man's cellphone next to him on the bar. He was aware of this kind of narrative. A hopeful, awkward tale told by a wronged man, the ragged edges smoothed out and punctuated by "it's nothing." He knew the tale because he'd told it himself over and over again in the past month. To colleagues and friends. To anyone who would listen. "Tamara is going to let me come back. She just needs some space and some time. She's just angry but she'll cool down. It'll pass," he'd say.

"It'll pass," Aaron said, taking a long gulp.

"Of course."

"The girl in your book. What's her deal?"

"You don't want to hear about that."

"Sure. I always wanted to be a writer. I always thought that maybe I could write a book."

Charlie was used to this line, this idea that everyone had a book in them somewhere. Personally he thought that was bullshit, but was drunk and permissive and decided to humour him. "Just your typical failed love story. Guy wants girl, guy can't have girl."

"What's she like? Hot?"

"Well, I guess she's pretty simple. Nothing special. Pretty, but not beautiful. Interesting, but not fascinating. But he doesn't see that. For some reason he sees more. It's like he's been tricked. Like she's tricked him."

"Fuck, I hear that."

Aaron motioned the bartender back toward them.

"Round of shots please. Jack," he said with confidence. As if they were celebrating.

"I mean, she likes peach schnapps. Who likes peach schnapps?" Charlie mumbled absently, his head light with drink.

"Who does?"

"The girl. In my book."

"Veronica liked peach schnapps. Likes peach schnapps."

"Veronica?"

"Yeah. Veronica. She's my girl."

Charlie felt as if he had been punched in the chest. The fuzziness of alcohol lifted dramatically. Everything fell together quite suddenly, into a neat picture, and as the shot arrived and he downed it, a wave of panic overtook him suddenly, the kind of panic he recalled from his youth, when he was twenty and he wrote poems about conquests and hid out in bathrooms.

"Veronica. Pretty name. Will you excuse me for a moment?"

Charlie retreated to the bathroom, away from this boy who shared a bed with the girl he was convinced he loved. He swung open the stall door and without shutting it behind him collapsed to his knees, vomiting whisky with a guttural moan, his breathing strained, gagging, tears running down his face. He stared down at the filthy tiled floor, trying to figure out how to escape, what it meant, what he should do.

And then he realized. *She told him to leave.*

"So what did your girl do to you?"

Charlie splashed water on his face, composed himself, and went back out into the bar.

"Well, it was very nice to meet you, Aaron. If you'll excuse me, I have somewhere to be right now."

"Sure, no problem," Aaron said, surprised at Charlie's sudden departure. "Well, nice to meet you too. Good luck with your girl."

"Yeah, you too."

CHAPTER SIXTY-THREE

In the book Charlie could have Ronnie. She could be his.

He could have her and he could fuck her.

In the book there would be no Aaron.

No two-bedroom apartment in Parkdale. No wedding.

There would be no Tamara.

No Noah.

No writing career.

No disgusting first-year students with their poor hygiene and manuscripts and questions. No cocktail parties.

No accusations.

No anxiety.

In the book there would be no tests.

No cancer.

No too many whisky shots.

No lying and cheating and sneaking around.

No disasters.

No mistakes.

In the book there would be no book. Only Ronnie, with her Vivien Leigh, Elizabeth Taylor hair and her simplicity. The curve of her hip. Her mouth. Her offering of escape from a life Charlie had grown tired of. A life, that because of Ronnie, had disintegrated completely.

All Charlie had now was the book.

CHAPTER SIXTY-FOUR

Ronnie was in the bathtub, just as Lisa had instructed, contemplating where she would go and what she would do now that Aaron was gone and the wedding was off. Quitting her job and selling her things was as far as she'd gotten in the scenario that would get her out of her life in Toronto. She knew she couldn't stay and suffer the shame of the wedding cancellation, the concerned faces, the disappointment, that inevitable call from her mother where she would be worried about Ronnie's age, how hard it would be to find someone else, the shared knowledge that Ronnie had failed at the process of being a woman. Again.

She was considering ideas of distant locales . . . the places to escape that she and Charlie had discussed over and over as pipe dreams, places she could actually go now that she was free . . . when there was banging on the front door.

Ramona jolted from her light sleep on the blue bathmat next to the tub and galloped like a bull to the front door, letting out small, passive barks as she did. Generally Ronnie ignored the front door, assuming it was children raising money or adults selling worthless things, but it was an incessant, frantic pounding, and she could only assume it was Aaron, a few drinks in and without his keys.

She wrapped a white bath towel around herself and positioned Ramona between her and the front door, just in case it wasn't a fragile, emotional Aaron hellbent on making things right. She pulled it open slightly, leaving the chain lock on.

"You kicked him out."

"Oh fuck, Charlie. What are you doing here?"

"You kicked him out."

"You reek of whisky."

"Well, I've been having a drink with a friend and he let me know that you called off the wedding."

"What friend? What are you talking about? Charlie, I told you I didn't want to see you. Go back to your wife."

"My wife?" Charlie was aggressive in a way that disturbed Ronnie, a part of him she hadn't seen, likely provoked by too much whisky. He started laughing. "Go back to my wife? You've seen to the fact that'll never happen again. What did you tell her when she came to see you at work? Did you tell her I loved you, Ronnie? Did you tell her you were the only one I ever loved?"

"How did you find out about that?"

"It took her awhile, but Tamara told me that she managed to pull it out of you during a fucking haircut."

"Please. Don't blame me for that."

"Who would you like me to blame, then?"

"I think you should go. Call me tomorrow and we can talk like adults."

"Ronnie, I had a drink with Aaron."

Ronnie was silent. Bile filled her throat. She took a few steps back from the door and unlocked the chain . . . a gesture that Charlie should step inside. Despite the fact that she knew he was angry and she was slightly afraid of him in a way she hadn't been in the past, she wanted him out of the doorway where he risked having the neighbours hear any more than they already had.

"Does he know?"

"No, Ronnie. He doesn't know. I, unlike you, was kind enough to spare him that truth."

"Well, at least he didn't accost you at your place of work."

"No, he stumbled into my hotel. The hotel where I now live,

thanks to you. Your Aaron bought the stranger at the end of the bar a drink so they could cheers their sorrows."

"Oh fuck."

"Oh, don't worry. Your careful illusion isn't shattered. I'm just the random stranger he talked to at a hotel lobby bar about his girl Veronica. And he just thinks you have cold feet. Do you have cold feet?"

"No."

"Then you're leaving him?"

"I don't know."

"You don't know? *My life is fucking ruined*, and you don't know?"

"That's not my fault, Charlie. You ruined your own life."

"I can't believe you. I can't believe I loved you."

"All I know is that I don't want all of you dictating my life anymore."

"Fuck you, Ronnie. I never tried to dictate anything. You're toxic. Poisonous."

"You held me hostage." Ronnie was yelling now, holding the towel tightly around her while tears fell freely down her cheeks. "You made me love you and you were never, ever going to leave her. And I knew that and I just followed along. That day at your front door? When you looked at me like you didn't even know me?"

"There was nothing I could have done. You know that."

"There was so much you could have done. You knew that you were never going to leave and you just let me follow along. It can't be you or him anymore. It has to be me."

Charlie softened, took a few steps toward her, reached out his arm, attempted to touch her cheek "But, Ronnie—"

"No, Charlie. I need you to go. You're scaring me," she said, pushing his hand away and clutching the towel closer with the other hand.

But Charlie wasn't listening. He put his arm around her waist and pulled her toward him. She resisted meekly at first, and then with more of her strength, but he began kissing her face, her mouth . . . clumsily, awkwardly . . . while she tried to pull away.

"But I love you, Ronnie. I left my family for you. I gave everything up. I lost Noah. I sacrificed it all for you."

"Stop it. Stop—"

"I love you, Ronnie. Come back to me. Please. Please come back."

"Please. Stop."

But Charlie wouldn't stop. He yanked the towel from her body, grabbed at her naked body, still damp from the bath, pulling her down to the floor as she kicked and squirmed. He was then firmly on top of her, gripping her wrists to prevent escape, bruising elbows, wrists, and knees against the hardwood floor.

"Charlie, please stop. Please. Don't."

"But you always liked it this way. Didn't you?"

She turned her head as he tried kiss her. He let go of one of her wrists to put his hand between her bare legs. Forced his fingers inside her as she clawed at him.

She decided to plead. Cried out. "Charlie, please. Please. Please don't do this. Please."

"But you're mine, Ronnie. You're mine."

"You don't want to do this."

He took a moment to look down at her, looked down at her body exposed beneath him, suddenly catching sight of a long pink scar on her abdomen, a cut fresh and healing, a new marking he had not seen before on a body he'd studied endlessly, worshipped limitlessly.

He realized it had been done. That while they had been apart it had been done.

He froze, the sight of it there revealing the reality of what he was doing.

"Oh, Ronnie. I . . . when? Why didn't you tell me?"

It was then that Charlie felt a searing pain in his right calf. A tearing, excruciating, severing anguish through the flesh and muscle, through his entire body. He looked behind him to find that Ramona had latched her massive jaw just beneath the back of his right knee and into his right calf. Once she had a secure grip, she began shaking her head back and forth as if she had found a small animal to dismember. Charlie let out a deep, inhuman groan, lifting himself off Ronnie and attempting to kick the frenzied dog off him with his uninjured leg.

Ronnie scrambled for the towel, wrapping it around herself and getting a safe distance from Charlie.

"For god's sake, Ronnie. Call her off me." The words were barely audible, so marred by agonizing pain.

Ronnie waited a moment, watched wordlessly as Ramona twist-ed and thrashed, and then called out the dog's name, gesturing for her to come. She wrapped her arms around the anxious, frustrated animal, attempting to control her as Ramona lunged and snarled. She strategically positioned the dog between herself and Charlie.

"Charlie, I need you to go. Now." Ronnie wasn't crying any-more. She was stoic. Charlie's leg was throbbing, and blood was be-ginning to seep through his pants, spreading down toward his ankle and onto the floor of the hallway. He looked like a wounded animal, crumpled in on himself in a way that suggested he had given up.

"Ronnie . . ."

"Don't say anything, Charlie. Just leave. I can't even look at you."

"I didn't mean . . . oh god, I'm so sorry," Charlie started, horrified.

"Just fucking go."

Ramona barked.

"Can't you at least give me something to stop the bleeding?" he asked, a final request in a situation he knew he could not fix.

Ronnie stood up, letting go of the dog but gesturing for her to stay. She pulled the towel from her body, holding it out with a single swift gesture. She stood there completely naked, scarred, tear-streaked, and defiant, with the Rottweiler standing menacingly beside her, its muzzle faintly pink with Charlie's blood.

"Now get the fuck out of here. I never, ever want to see you again."

(CHAPTER SIXTY-FIVE)

Aaron checked out of the hotel the next morning, gleefully optimistic. He had spent the evening in a blissful two-whisky sleep, dreamless and stretched out in the rare comfort of a night alone in a king-sized bed.

Full of confidence he came home to find that Ronnie had, as promised, left.

There was a faint red stain on the hardwood in the front hallway, a bloodstained towel in the hamper, and a note that said only "Please take care of Ramona while I am gone."

Aaron found the dog cowering shamefully on their bed, as if she had done some secret thing, something terrible and wrong.

Aaron read the words "while I am gone" over and over and over, wondering if they meant she was coming back.

CHAPTER SIXTY-SIX

Ronnie had spent her life being taken care of. Tongue depressors and paper gowns, she was the focal point of a world of worry, a broken thing that needed to be taken care of.

I didn't want to be forgiven.
I felt like I'd gotten off too easy.
I simply walked away.
The pain?
I felt like I deserved it.
And it was the only thing that made me feel better.
Because I get away with everything.
I've always been getting away with everything.

What Ronnie needed now was darkness. She needed the sun and the stars and the moon blotted out for a time, at the very least so she could convince herself that a way would be found. That she could survive without the care, without the good and the bad. Without the violence of her desires. That she could feel alive without the turmoil.

Ronnie went to stay with Lisa. She called her immediately after Charlie left. It took Lisa a good fifteen minutes through the mangled, hysterical sobs to understand what had happened.

"Listen to me, Ronnie. Just pack some things. Let Ramona out and then put her in the bedroom for the night. I'll stop by and get her first thing tomorrow morning. I'm calling a cab to come now and pick you up."

The cab arrived as promised and Ronnie spent that night

drinking the entire contents of Lisa's minimal liquor cabinet. When she had enough she ended up in Lisa's lap, crying and lamenting while Lisa stroked her hair. When she finally passed out Lisa put a Bay blanket over her on the couch, and switched off the light.

The next morning, Ronnie sat puffy-eyed and defeated at the kitchen table while the two had breakfast (a fried egg on rye toast with hot sauce). She hadn't changed her clothes, nor did she feel any reason to do so. Lisa immediately let her know she could stay as long as she needed to. "If you need anything from home I'll go and get it for you."

"Just Ramona."

"The two of you are more than welcome."

"You don't have to do this, you know. I'll figure something out."

"I wouldn't mind the company. And if you decide you want to stay, I wouldn't mind the help with the rent," she said, smiling.

"That's what you're supposed to say."

"Do I strike you as the kind of person who would ever say something she didn't mean? Please."

Lisa's apartment in Kensington Market was comforting in its perfected lack of domesticity, the very opposite of everything Aaron had been striving for. There was a ceramic Elvis head in the living room and framed prints of sugar skulls on the walls, and a healthy littering of papers, take-out containers, and a collection of abandoned glasses with their remnants crusting and congealing inside. Despite the state of it, the apartment was actually quite spacious, with a very small office space that was functioning as a closet for endless piles of Lisa's clothes.

"If you decide to stay, we can put a bed in there," Lisa offered, smiling.

The whole scene was comforting to Ronnie, the neighbourhood

allowing her to wander and regain her footing with minor milestones like grocery shopping and having a coffee by herself.

"If there's anything I know how to deal with it's breakups," Lisa said. "It's *America's Next Top Model* downloads and buffalo wings for the rest of the week. I think you need to be as drunk as possible for most of the time, and I'm more than happy to facilitate that. I'll tell the salon you've got some stomach bug and you can't come in for the rest of the week, okay?"

"You know, I really appreciate this, Lisa."

"Really, it's no problem. Tell me about Stern's penis and consider us even."

Ronnie laughed for the first time in weeks. Lisa reached for her hand and squeezed it, her face uncharacteristically soft.

"You don't have to answer this if you don't want to. Fuck, you don't have to tell me anything at all if you don't want to—"

"No, I'm happy to talk to you about it." Ronnie wasn't really sure how true that was but was willing to find out.

"Why did you leave Aaron?"

"You mean besides the fact that I was having an affair with someone else?" Ronnie laughed again.

"Well, it's not like he knew. And given who you were having an affair with, it's not like he would find out."

"I love your brand of logic."

"No, seriously."

"I guess I just got sick of being taken care of."

"Well, then why didn't you stay with Charlie? Now that his wife knows?"

While she said that Charlie had come over to confront her, Ronnie didn't tell Lisa what Charlie had done. She would never tell anyone about it. She simply pushed it from her mind as quickly as she could. If she was honest with herself she would have realized that she felt like she had deserved it.

"I guess I just got sick of taking care of someone else."

Lisa began collecting dishes from the kitchen table and walked them over to the sink, adding them to the accumulating pile. "Well, let's take care of ourselves, shall we?"

(CHAPTER SIXTY-SEVEN)

"Charles, I really do believe it has great potential. It's the most optimistic, hopeful thing you've ever written. Truly romantic. Quite beautiful. You should be very proud."

Charlie took another long swig of his whisky, enjoying the satisfying clink of the ice against the glass as he returned it to the table.

His agent, a short, balding, likely impotent man who was gifted at both his profession and portraying unrealistic enthusiasm, was enabling him by picking up the tab at the Four Seasons hotel bar, the only reasonable hotel that Charlie could think of that he and Ronnie hadn't frequented.

They hadn't seen each other in a while, certainly not since Charlie's life had begun to fabulously unravel, and although it was clearly evident that it had, what with the beard he had cultivated and the vague smell of a lonely, single man coming off him, his agent acknowledged nothing—just gushed almost too enthusiastically about his finally completed novel.

"This one could be really profitable for you, Charles. A comeback."

Charlie didn't know he had something to come back from. He considered whether or not it was appropriate to order another drink at two in the afternoon.

"It'll do quite well with women, I'm sure," his agent added.

Charlie laughed loudly. "At least something will."

"Excuse me?"

Charlie waved him off and gestured to the bartender to bring him another. The agent raised his eyebrow slightly at the request but said nothing.

Despite all the enthusiasm, Charlie cared very little for the book and viewed it as a throwaway—hundreds and hundreds of pages documenting a life he didn't, couldn't have with Ronnie. He had only sent it because there was little else he could do.

"All I'm saying is I think this might be it for you. This might be the one. I think we should probably move on it quickly."

"Listen, do you think maybe you could lend me some money?"

An awkward pause and then a sympathetic look. "Are you and Tamara having problems?"

"Actually, never mind. We're fine."

The tab was paid care of his agency and the two shared a firm handshake, an agreement of enthusiastic potential, before Charlie limped off toward the lobby of a hotel much fancier than the one he was currently maxing out his credit card to stay in.

"Oh, and Charles?" the agent called after him.

Charlie turned, slightly dizzy from the drink.

"Give my best to Tamara and Noah."

CHAPTER SIXTY-EIGHT

Ronnie received an email from Tamara a month or so after she had moved into Lisa's apartment.

Lisa had left the invitation for Ronnie to stay open-ended and it had been working well, despite the fact that Ronnie had been sleeping on the couch and living out of a tiny bag. Occasionally she would return to the apartment in Parkdale to retrieve a few things, but she was in a holding pattern, largely undecided about what she would ultimately do.

"Don't sweat it, Rons," Lisa would say, lighting a joint. "Take all the time you need. I'm liking the company. And no one is saying you have to decide anything just yet."

One morning she was hungover, as she often was now, wandering around the one-bedroom plus den in her pyjamas, trying to feel vaguely human, when the email notification dinged from the computer in the corner.

She hoped it was Aaron. Then she hoped it was Charlie.

Veronica,

I would like to have dinner with you. Meet me at Coco Lezzone on College at 7 p.m. on Thursday evening. No anger. No blame.

I just want to understand.

Tamara

Ronnie asked for the time off when she started her shift that afternoon.

"So what was it about him? Why did you pick him?" Tamara asked. She'd had a few glasses of wine at this point, and apparently the pleasantries were over.

"I don't know what you mean," Ronnie said, buttering a slice of baguette with slow, deliberate precision. It had taken a good half an hour for her to get comfortable with being at dinner with Tamara, but early on in the evening, almost immediately, Tamara has assured her this wasn't about blame. And now that Ronnie had ejected both Charlie and Aaron from her life, she didn't really feel she had anything to lose.

"I mean, I know why I picked him. But why did you pick him?'

"But I didn't pick him. I just met him. I told you. At a party."

"I remember that party. I think I was watching Noah that night."

"It was just a stupid moment. A mistake."

"But that's never the way this kind of thing works. When I met him I picked him. I saw him onstage reading one of those stupid poems and I picked him," Tamara said.

Ronnie didn't know this detail of Tamara's first meeting with Charlie, found it hard to comprehend that this woman had been enamoured enough with his performance, so many years ago, to chase after him.

"Honestly. It was a few seconds. A few glasses. Whisky and wine. He pursued me."

"Oh, Veronica. You must have been ready for him to show up. And he was certainly ready to fuck you."

"I don't like the way this is going," Ronnie said, uncomfortable.

She hadn't taken a bite of her bread and was holding it awkwardly. "I understand your impulse to understand. But please don't belittle it for me."

"Fine. Maybe not fuck you. But need you. He needed something else. I understand that now."

"That's generous of you, considering."

"I just mean that you may not have known you needed him. To end your relationship with Aaron. But you did. Just like he needed you to end our marriage." Tamara's face softened as she said this. She seemed pleased with her conclusion, and Ronnie submitted a weak nod.

"Does that mean you're glad it happened, then?"

"The affair?" Tamara laughed and put her glass down on the table with some force. "No one wants their husband to sleep with someone ten years younger than them." She laughed lightly.

"Of course not."

"But yes, I'm glad it's over. I was growing tired of . . ."

"Taking care of him?" Ronnie stopped herself. "Sorry. I have a nasty habit of finishing people's sentences."

"No. It's okay. You're right. I was tired of being the better one."

"Do you think you were?"

"Of course not. But we all have our roles to play and they get exhausting after a while."

"I can sympathize with that. And I'm very sure Aaron feels the exact same way."

"Ronnie, you are nothing like Charlie. Charlie is a child. There was a time he couldn't even ride the subway. You can't even comprehend what it's like to be with someone like . . ." Tamara paused, realizing that of course Ronnie could understand. "Well. Maybe you were better at it than I was. A better person than I am."

Tamara is good.

"It was just new and it was just something else. An escape. I was no better. Just different. He loved you. He loves you. He'll always . . ."

"I don't need you to say that. I know that. He just wanted you more."

"But he didn't. He wouldn't leave you. He refused."

"Did you ask?"

"Not at first. But then it was all I could think about. Every day. I think at first you think you can cope with it. You can handle the fact that there's someone else."

"Um, sorry, but I think in this case you were the 'someone else.'"

"Fair. Yes. I just mean . . . who he goes home to. That he shares a bed with. That is his whole world." Tamara laughed bitterly at this comment but Ronnie gracefully chose to ignore her. "You accept all that. But then it settles in that you will never completely have him. And you get greedy."

"It's strange, he was a much better husband the year the two of you were . . ." Tamara stopped herself. She couldn't bring herself to finish and Ronnie didn't push.

Ronnie changed the subject. "How is Noah? I mean, now that Charlie is gone?'

"You know, I want to say he's not coping very well, but with Noah you can't tell. He's always not coping well. And in some ways, he does seem calmer now that Charlie is gone. I don't want to say that Charlie was a bad father. He was a really good father. But he was always so wrung out. I feel like Noah knew it. Didn't like the energy. I think Noah is more intuitive than people give him credit for."

"Sure."

"I'm sorry about what happened to you, Ronnie. Charlie told me. About you being sick."

"I appreciate that. It was Aaron who wanted to have children, anyway. For me it was all wrapped up in expectation."

"Where you're so focused on what everyone else wants that you can't even figure out what it was you wanted when you started."

"There must have been a time when things were good between the two of you. The three of you. A time you look back on," Ronnie said. She knew full well she was reaching for something positive, some sort of happy snapshot she could hang up so she could feel like Charlie had redeeming qualities. That he wasn't the monster who was attacked by her Rottweiler in her front hall.

"Marriage is strange like that. You can't really understand it unless you're in it. The feelings of right now always seem to be magnified. They overshadow everything else. Now, I can't even remember a time when we were happy."

"He used to talk about how happy you were. How lucky he was."

"You're lying. I appreciate it, but you are."

"No. It's true," she said, even though she was.

"He was happy. With you. He found someone new to take care of him when I grew tired of it. I was never happy. But I think I knew, deep down, there was someone else that was—we weren't even sleeping together anymore."

"I'm sorry," Ronnie said, bowing her head slightly. The waiter arrived with their meals, both pasta with bolognese sauce on account of the fact that Ronnie was so nervous she was only able to repeat Tamara's order. While he ground pepper on their meals and offered them parmesan Tamara looked away awkwardly, and when he left she looked directly at Ronnie.

"The sex. How was it?"

"Tamara, don't. You don't want to . . ."

"Yes I do. Was it passionate? Was it rough? Did he . . ."

"It was good. Yes," Ronnie said meekly.

"Do you miss it?"

"Please, don't."

"All right. Do you miss him?"

There was a long pause between them, their plates steaming, their glasses approaching empty.

"More than anything."

(ACKNOWLEDGEMENTS)

Thanks to the wonderful folks at ECW for their investment and care, especially Jen Hale and Jen Knoch for their invaluable editorial commitment and direction. I'm additionally eternally grateful to Samantha Haywood for being a patient and supportive agent and friend, without whom so much of my work wouldn't be possible.

Thanks to the Banff Centre for offering a refuge for the completion of the manuscript, and to Jared Bland and Robert J. Wiersema for selflessly reading early drafts and offering invaluable editorial guidance. Thanks to the wonderful team at *The Walrus*, who over the years have become more like family than colleagues, and to Mark Medley at the *National Post* for his generosity and faith.

I'm forever indebted to Dani, Nat, and Panic for the kind of loyalty and friendship I never before would have believed possible, and to my parents for their unwavering support, even when they were unsure what path I was on.

And as always, thank you to Spencer, who with each passing day proves to be the best decision I ever made.

227

STACEY MAY FOWLES is a writer and magazine professional living in Toronto. Her first novel, *Be Good*, was published by Tightrope Books in 2007. *This Magazine* called it "probably the most finely realized small press novel to come out of Canada in the last year," and film rights have been optioned by Federgreen Entertainment Inc. In fall 2008 she released an illustrated novel, *Fear of Fighting*, and staged a theatrical adaptation of it with Nightwood Theatre. The novel was later selected as a *National Post* Canada Also Reads pick for 2010. Her writing has appeared in various magazines and journals, including *The Walrus*, *Maisonneuve*, *Quill & Quire*, *Taddle Creek*, *Hazlitt*, and *Prism*. She has been anthologized in *Nobody Passes: Rejecting the Rules of Gender and Conformity*, *Yes Means Yes*, and PEN Canada's *Finding the Words*. Most recently, she co-edited the anthology *She's Shameless: Women Write About Growing Up, Rocking Out, and Fighting Back*. She is a regular contributor to the *National Post* books section, and currently works at *The Walrus*.

At ECW Press, we want you to enjoy this book in whatever format you like, whenever you like. Leave your print book at home and take the eBook to go! Purchase the print edition and receive the eBook free. Just send an email to ebook@ecwpress.com and include:

- the book title
- the name of the store where you purchased it
- your receipt number
- your preference of file type: PDF or ePub?

A real person will respond to your email with your eBook attached. And thanks for supporting an independently owned Canadian publisher with your purchase!